## Nothing She Had Ever Done Had Been So Difficult.

"What I'm trying to say, Mikhail, is that before our relationship goes any further, you should give yourself the opportunity to meet other women. You may find you don't feel for me the way you think you do."

"You want me to go out with other women?"

"Y-yes . . ."

Mikhail's eyes flashed. "I would never have imagined that you were capable of this, Erin. If you wanted to break off with me, you had only to say so. At least I wouldn't have lost respect for you as I have now."

To Erin there was only one explanation for Mikhail's behavior: He could never have felt for her as she did for him.

---

**MAURA SEGER**

has been writing stories since childhood but has only recently made it a full-time career. She traveled widely as a child, and this is reflected in the many locales of her novels. She married after a whirlwind courtship that ~~could have~~ been taken from a ~~novel. She~~ credits her husband's ~~sense of~~ humor with helping ~~her realize her~~ dream of being a wri~~ter.~~

Dear Reader,

Silhouette Special Editions are an exciting new line of contemporary romances from Silhouette Books. Special Editions are written specifically for our readers who want a story with heightened romantic tension.

Special Editions have all the elements you've enjoyed in Silhouette Romances and *more*. These stories concentrate on romance in a longer, more realistic and sophisticated way, and they feature greater sensual detail.

I hope you enjoy this book and all the wonderful romances from Silhouette.

Karen Solem
Editor-in-Chief
Silhouette Books

# MAURA SEGER
# A Gift
# Beyond Price

*Silhouette Special Edition*
Published by Silhouette Books New York
**America's Publisher of Contemporary Romance**

SILHOUETTE BOOKS, a Division of Simon & Schuster, Inc.
1230 Avenue of the Americas, New York, N.Y. 10020

Copyright © 1983 by Seger, Inc.

Distributed by Pocket Books

ISBN: 0-671-53635-4

First Silhouette Books printing December, 1983

10 9 8 7 6 5 4 3 2 1

Map by Ray Lundgren

SILHOUETTE, SILHOUETTE SPECIAL EDITION and
colophon are registered trademarks of Simon & Schuster, Inc.

America's Publisher of Contemporary Romance

Printed in the U.S.A.

# A Gift
# Beyond Price

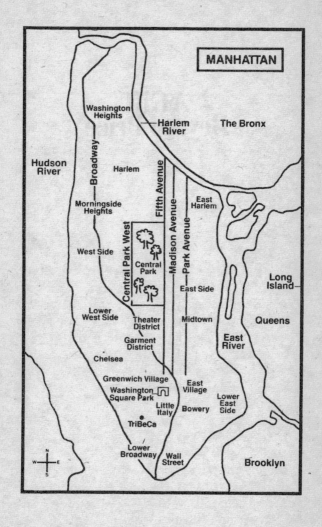

# Chapter One

"What'sa matter, lady? Waitin' fer a color ye like?"

Erin Hennessey glared at the driver behind her. The traffic light guarding one of Kennedy Airport's overcrowded parking lots had just turned green, but harassed motorists were already blaring their horns.

She sighed resignedly. After five years in New York she should be used to the frenetic pace. A rueful smile curved her generous mouth as she reflected that the City's high-pressure environment was a large part of its attraction.

There were times when she missed the gentler, more natural rhythms of life on her parents' Wyoming ranch, but she wouldn't have traded her life in New York and her career with *Focus*—the national news magazine that made almost as many headlines as it reported—for anything.

Squeezing into a spot between a behemoth convertible and a garishly painted panel truck, Erin glanced at her watch. Ten minutes to four. The Air France jet carrying Mikhail Demertov from Paris to New York would be making its final approach.

Outside the International Arrivals Building a tall, gaily decorated Christmas tree added an unusually joyful touch. Erin's large green eyes widened slightly as she noticed it. The events of the last few days had banished all thoughts of the coming holidays from her mind.

Since learning that Mikhail Demertov had been freed, she had found it impossible to concentrate on anything else. Even as she entered the cavernous terminal she could hardly believe that in just a short time she would be meeting the man whose writing she had admired for years and whose freedom from an East European prison was in large part due to her own efforts.

The flashing arrivals monitor indicated that the Air France flight was on time. Standing at one of the wide plate-glass windows overlooking the runways, Erin watched the jet taxi to its gate. It would take at least half an hour for the passengers to leave the plane and begin clearing customs. Her stomach tightened with impatience, but no outward sign ruffled the cool, calm exterior she presented to the world.

Her shoulder-length auburn hair was swept into a neat twist at the back of her well-shaped head. The dank December wind had loosened a few feathery tendrils that did nothing to detract from the elegance of smooth, apricot-tinted skin, slender yet strong features set off by expressive emerald eyes, and her surprisingly sensual mouth hinting at facets of her character usually kept under rigorous control.

She was simply dressed in a camel's-hair pantsuit whose austerely elegant lines were lightened by a soft moss-green turtleneck. The well-tailored outfit set off the long, slim line of her body, while not quite concealing the gentle swell of high, firm breasts.

At twenty-eight, Erin had come a long way from the naive girl who had arrived in New York with a head full of dreams and very little practical grasp of how to achieve them, but she had lost none of the vibrant intelligence and warm good nature that first won her an entry into journalism. Though on the outside she might appear strictly professional, concerned only with getting the job done, on the inside she could still feel as deeply as ever about the injustices of the world and their victims.

It was that ability to care about other people less fortunate than herself that was responsible for her being at Kennedy Airport on a blustery December day, waiting for a man she had never met but nonetheless felt she knew well.

Too tense to sit down, Erin prowled the corridor outside the customs area thinking about Mikhail Demertov. Few men knew as much about injustice or were as willing to speak out against it, regardless of personal danger.

At thirty-two the brilliant East European writer

already had a worldwide reputation. Published secretly in his homeland, his books were a clarion call to freedom. The "Demertov Papers," as they had come to be known, were heralded around the world as a testimony to human courage and determination.

He had paid a heavy price for his convictions. Hunted for years by his country's secret police, he had lived in basements and attics while keeping constantly on the move. Despite desperate efforts to protect him, his whereabouts had finally been betrayed. For the past year Mikhail had been in a labor camp near the Arctic Circle, suffering deprivations few could even imagine.

The Western news media had covered the Demertov story in depth, but it was Erin's acutely sensitive, moving articles for *Focus* that transformed an international celebrity into a person millions of people felt they knew as well as the members of their own families, and which had finally convinced his country's leaders to use him as a bargaining chip in their efforts to negotiate more favorable trade agreements.

In her brown leather shoulder bag was a copy of the only known photo of the man Erin was waiting to meet. Taken nine years before it showed a young, handsome intellectual with aristocratic features beneath his short blond hair and a tall, rangy body that looked as though it had not quite grown into itself.

Glancing toward the doors of the customs area, Erin wondered how much of that young man remained. After the hardships and brutality he had endured, Mikhail could be expected to have lost the

confident enthusiasm she sensed in the photo. If his
years as a fugitive hadn't done so, then his experiences in the labor camp must surely have made him
hard and embittered.

She bit her lip as she wondered, not for the first
time, just how well equipped she was to welcome
such a man to his new country and how she could
help him adjust to a totally foreign way of life.

But if she didn't do it, who would? Some anonymous functionary from the State Department, concerned only with looking good to his superiors? Or
well-meaning but self-centered political groups, who
would see Mikhail as a useful rallying point? Or
media stars, who wouldn't hesitate to exploit his
newsworthy appeal?

None of them seemed equipped to provide what a
man just hurled from his homeland and the misery
of prison into a completely different world would
need. Granted, her own motives weren't completely
selfless. Erin hoped to round off her coverage of the
Demertov story with a personal, exclusive interview.
But she was most concerned with helping Mikhail
adjust to freedom so that he would be able to keep
on writing and fulfill the immense potential shown in
his earlier works.

A stream of people began to exit the customs area
to be welcomed by eager friends and relatives.
Standing a little apart from the busy scene, Erin
craned her neck to get a look inside the huge room,
where a few unlucky travelers were unpacking their
belongings at low tables while most were waved
through with just a few questions.

Erin breathed a silent prayer that Mikhail would not be detained. What an introduction it would be to his new country if he were held back by overeager officials anxious to rifle through his few belongings.

She needn't have worried. The man who stepped through the automatic doors a moment later looked far too tired and dazed to be concerned with anything other than putting one foot in front of the other.

It took her an instant to realize who he was, because Mikhail Demertov bore little resemblance to his photograph. In one sense his experiences had dealt harshly with him, etching deep lines into his face and adding a grim set to his mouth. But in another, far more potent way, they had magnified his innate strength and masculinity to a remarkable degree.

Her breath caught in her throat. Struck by the sheer impact of male grace and power unlike anything she had ever before experienced, she struggled vainly to achieve her usual reporter's objectivity.

The years had widened the broad sweep of his shoulders and chest and toughened the long, sinewy lines of his legs. Not an ounce of fat marred his lean, hard body or softened his features.

Beneath tousled blond hair shot through with silver, his gray eyes were deeply set. Chiseled cheekbones emphasized the ruggedness of his features and highlighted the bronze of his skin. He wore a full beard that, coupled with his casual dress and the duffel bag slung over his shoulder, gave him the look of another, simpler age. He might have been a Viking home from the sea instead of a man just released from hell.

Only the shuttered blankness of his gaze hinted at what he had suffered. Though he was clearly close to exhaustion, he was still wary. Studying him, Erin was reminded of a dangerous animal brought to bay but nonetheless ready to turn on its hunters and exact full measure from them.

That impression was strengthened as she approached him. Mikhail's back stiffened, further accentuating the vast difference in their heights. Erin was tall for a woman, but he towered over her. Slowly, giving him plenty of time to see it as a gesture of friendship, she held out her hand.

"I'm Erin Hennessey, Mr. Demertov. I'm very glad to meet you at last."

For a moment he continued to stare at her guardedly. Then some flicker of recognition lightened his eyes. A big, callused hand accepted hers.

"Forgive me, Miss Hennessey. Of course, I knew you were planning to be here, but I didn't expect anyone so young or so . . . striking."

The deep timbre of his voice seemed to resonate within Erin. A faint blush stained her cheeks. Whatever she had expected from this man, it wasn't courtly compliments. She was acutely aware of the warmth of his hand, which was still holding hers. Forced to look up at him, she was struck by the intensity of the smoky gray eyes moving over her with undisguised interest.

Recalling herself with difficulty, Erin freed her hand. "I—I'm sure you're anxious to get some rest. My car is just outside. . . ."

Still staring at her, Mikhail nodded. He shifted the duffel bag more comfortably on his shoulder as they made their way through the milling crowd.

Erin was silent until they reached her car. All the careful, reassuring things she had meant to say were now beyond her. A swift readjustment in her thinking was clearly essential.

When she was approached about taking charge of Mikhail Demertov and guiding him through his first difficult weeks in his new country, Erin hadn't hesitated to agree. The suggestion from her editor at *Focus* had made perfect sense, and the thought of helping a man whose work she intensely admired had banished any small doubt she might have had.

Now, barely five minutes after meeting him, Erin understood the ridiculousness of thinking anyone could "take charge" of Mikhail. He had come through an experience that would have destroyed most men, and with his self-command and virility vividly intact. The situation suddenly had ramifications she had not even begun to consider.

Mikhail dropped his bag into the trunk of the car, then paused before settling into the passenger seat. He stood, tall and agile, looking out over the lighted ribbons of highway leading toward the city's diamond-splattered skyline. Again Erin had the impression of an immensely powerful, proud animal, this time surveying its new territory before taking possession. She even thought she heard a low growl of satisfaction as he slid into the car.

Within the confines of the compact car his presence became even more overwhelming. Maneuvering into traffic, she glanced at him surreptitiously. He was leaning back against the headrest, his eyes half closed. Long legs stretched out in front of him, the worn denim emphasizing the taut muscles of his thighs. Despite his relaxed pose he was clearly attentive to everything going on around him.

Realizing that he did not intend to sleep, Erin asked, "Were there any problems with customs?"

Mikhail smiled faintly. "None at all. I got the impression that stateless persons traveling on U.N. passports come through here everyday."

That couldn't possibly be the case, but Erin was still grateful to the anonymous functionaries who, in the finest tradition of New Yorkers, considered it a matter of honor never to express surprise at anything. Even the arrival of a man expelled from his native land, stripped of his citizenship and protected only by the offer of political asylum would warrant nothing more than a raised eyebrow.

"As far as the next few days go," she went on tentatively, "I thought you'd just want to rest and get your bearings. Perhaps have a checkup. . . ."

She broke off, not anxious to dwell on the possible aftereffects of his experience. Having envisioned all sorts of physical problems that would require immediate medical attention, she was greatly relieved to find Mikhail apparently healthy, but she didn't underestimate the emotional scars he must bear. No one could endure so much without paying some price.

"I don't need a doctor," he informed her flatly. "Some decent food and shelter will be more than enough. If I had been in the camp a few more months it might have been a different story, but, as it is, I am very fortunate."

He didn't elaborate, and Erin made no effort to draw him out. She knew few survived the prison camps with their bodies and spirits intact. When Mikhail had been only a distant figure in her mind, the thought of what he was suffering had been painful enough. But now that she saw him as a real, flesh-and-blood man, she instinctively shied away from images of his past.

"This is a new experience for me," she admitted softly. "Normally our State Department would help you get settled. They're good at their job, but they're also very . . . impersonal. Since *Focus* helped to secure your release my editor got the government to agree that we would also assist with your adjustment here. However, if you would prefer a different arrangement . . . ?"

She unconsciously held her breath as she waited for his reply, then let it go when he said, "Not at all. I have every confidence that you will take excellent care of me, Miss Hennessey."

What was it about this man that gave him the ability to make her blush more in the last hour than she had in years? His drawling pronunciation of her name hinted at the extent of the "care" he might be anticipating. As she glanced at him worriedly, Erin was surprised by his unbridled grin. With a start she realized that this man, who only forty-eight hours before had been serving a life sentence at hard labor under the most grueling conditions, was still strong and secure enough to be teasing her.

Relieved, she matched his smile with her own. "And I have every confidence you won't hesitate to let me know if I make a mistake, Mr. Demertov."

He laughed softly. "Since neither of us has been through anything like this before, I suppose we will work it out together. For my part, I have no immediate plans beyond getting some sleep and finding my bearings. After that I will have to think about finding a place to live and begin the work I want to do. But, for the moment, I wish only to put my thoughts in order."

The fact that he was able to give any consideration at all to the future, and particularly to his writing, strengthened Erin's already considerable admiration for him. "About your work," she said softly, "you do plan to go on writing?"

He glanced at her quizzically. "Do you imagine I have a choice? The need to write is a living force inside me. For that reason alone I have been able to survive what would otherwise have certainly destroyed me."

He shook his head firmly. "It would be the greatest irony if freedom accomplished what all the repressions of my government could not. As soon as I am able, I will begin again to tell the story of my people and their suffering. But this time there will be no secret police to hide from, no government-controlled press to deny my words."

His big body moved slightly in the passenger seat, as though he were already rising to the challenge. "I will be truly free to think . . . to write . . . and, most importantly, to publish. That is as necessary to me as air and water."

Listening to him, Erin felt oddly humbled. On the surface she and the man beside her had a great deal in common. They were both writers who faced the injustices of the world with clarity and courage. Both wrote from deeply rooted convictions and an often unbearable sense of outrage.

But there the similarities ended. While Erin observed the sufferings of others with insight and compassion, Mikhail had actually lived them. For him, freedom was not some abstract ideal but a concrete force without which he could not endure. He might have enjoyed a comfortable, even luxurious existence in his own country if he had been willing to use his talents in the service of its repressive government. Instead, he had chosen to risk everything rather than give up his beliefs.

Curiosity about what motivated such a man surged through Erin, but she knew her questions should wait until he had a chance to regain his equilibrium. She turned her mind to easier thoughts. "I know before you began writing you did quite a lot c traveling. Did you get to New York?"

"No, this is one Western city I missed. In recent years my travel has been very restricted," Mikhail reminded her gently. "I have not been outside my own country since I was a teenager."

Yet he wrote with an understanding of human nature that transcended any single time or place. Keeping her tone light, Erin said, "Then perhaps, once you've rested, you'd like to play tourist. I'll be happy to show you around."

Mikhail nodded gravely. "Thank you. I would like that. If you will give me your phone number . . . ?"

"Actually, that won't be necessary. I thought . . . that is . . . if I were you, I wouldn't want to be staying in a hotel right now. My apartment is quite large. . . . You're welcome to use the guest room. . . . That is, unless you'd rather not."

She was putting it clumsily. What had seemed so simple when she had thought of Mikhail only as a highly intelligent, talented writer in need of help now appeared far more complex. Never had she imagined that she would be opening her home to such a potently male stranger.

"Your apartment will be fine," he said quietly. "I really wasn't looking forward to staying in a hotel."

He sounded so matter-of-fact that some of the tension eased from her. Surely there was no reason why two sensible adults couldn't share the same accommodations for a short time without becoming anything more than friends. Her neighbors wouldn't think twice about the arrangement unless they became aware of Mikhail's identity, and then they would only be excited to have such a renowned figure in their midst. That was one good thing about

New York, she thought wryly. No one cared about what anyone else did so long as they weren't too noisy about it.

Keeping her eyes on the road, Erin fought against a growing sense of unease. Her life so far had been relatively uncomplicated, with hard work leading to achievement and satisfaction. She had long ago grown accustomed to feeling very much in control of her own destiny.

Now that feeling was abruptly gone. The man beside her was an unknown quantity with the power to affect her in ways she couldn't begin to imagine. Created by experiences that were utterly alien to her, he had needs and objectives different from those of any other man she knew. His relentless strength of both body and will had already proven him capable of surmounting even the greatest obstacles. Already she sensed the potential for a clash between them growing out of the age-old confrontation between men and women. If that happened, she would have very little chance of emerging unscathed.

That knowledge at once frightened and excited her. She was shivering slightly as she pulled into the garage beneath her apartment house.

# Chapter Two

$\mathcal{D}$o all American writers live like this?" Mikhail asked, making no effort to hide his astonishment. He stood in the center of the large entry hall, staring ahead to the large windows overlooking the City's skyline. Below, the winter-bare expanse of Central Park stretched far into the distance. Through the caverns of residential and office buildings framing it on the other side, the East River gleamed dully.

"Very few," Erin admitted. "I was extremely lucky to find this co-op."

That was putting it mildly. She could still hardly believe her good fortune at being able to buy a home in one of the city's loveliest buildings. Only the determined generosity of an old-time reporter, who saw in Erin the daughter she'd never had, had made it possible. "I've got all the money I'll ever need," the woman had insisted shortly before she retired to live in the Caribbean. "But I'd like to know my home is being enjoyed by someone I have something in common with."

And enjoy it Erin did. She took pride in the high-ceilinged, airy rooms tastefully furnished with a personalized blend of antiques and contemporary pieces and highlighted by her small but select collection of pre–Colombian art. The style was uniquely her own, and the result was a warm, homey atmosphere that said a lot about the person who lived there.

Handwoven native American rugs were scattered across the parquet floors. Their muted earth tones complemented the polished veneers of the oak tables and bookcases. Low-slung modular units covered in unbleached cotton provided ample seating, even for the large parties she occasionally liked to give. A burled walnut desk stood in one corner of the living room. On the wall opposite it hung a vivid, star-pattern quilt. Large plants in wicker containers brought a welcome touch of green.

"In my country," Mikhail said, still looking around bemusedly, "this could only belong to a top government official."

Erin took a step closer to him, noticing how the powerful sweep of his back and shoulders blotted out the view. "*This* is your country now."

He turned, flashing her a sharply perceptive look.

"You are right, of course. But I think it will take a while for me to get used to the idea."

As he continued to stand in the entry hall, Erin took his hand. Gently she guided him into the cheerful country kitchen and sat him down at the butcher-block table. "I expect you're hungry. I'm not the world's greatest cook, but I can rustle up some steak and eggs. How does that sound?"

"Luxurious," Mikhail murmured dryly.

They spoke little as she prepared the meal, then not at all as he ate. His meticulous attention to the food brought home to her forcibly how much she had always taken for granted. He ate with the care usually reserved for gourmet feasts, but finished before the plate was empty.

"I'm sorry, but I'm full." A wry grin touched his mouth. "Perhaps in time I will be able to do justice to your cooking. It's better than you suggested."

Erin nodded silently. She should have realized he wouldn't be able to get through a regular meal until his stomach had a chance to adjust to such a relatively large quantity of food. As for her cooking, she considered him a less than discriminating audience, but hoped his palate would soon improve.

Stacking the dishwasher she said, "You must be tired. I'll get your bed ready."

After making use of the adjacent bath, Mikhail followed her into the guest room. He took in the large platform bed, well-stocked bookshelves and TV silently. After folding back the down-filled comforter, Erin turned to leave. However dazed and weary he might be, he was a grown man who definitely did not need tucking in.

At the door she paused. For all his unmistakable strength, Mikhail looked achingly vulnerable. His broad shoulders stooped slightly, and his eyes were shadowed with fatigue. Gently she said. "Sleep as late as you like. I'm taking the next few days off, so I'll be here to fix breakfast whenever you wake up."

So softly that she had to strain to hear him, he murmured, "Thank you, Erin. You are very kind."

She nodded mutely, closing the door before he could see the sudden sheen of tears in her emerald eyes.

Still too awake to consider sleeping, Erin wandered out to the living room. She selected a book at random and curled up on one of the couch units. For a few minutes she could hear faint sounds from the bedroom as Mikhail settled down. Then silence. She sighed faintly, hoping he would sleep well.

The book was a mystery she had wanted to read for some time, but not even its tense, fast-paced plot could hold her attention. Her thoughts remained on the man in the next room. In her years as a reporter she had met many different kinds of people in many different situations, but never had she reacted to anyone as strongly as she did to Mikhail. The near-awe she had felt for him as a writer was turning rapidly to admiration and attraction for what she saw in him as a man.

Telling herself it would be foolhardy to mistake natural sympathy for anything deeper, Erin tried again to concentrate on the book. She had gotten as far as the third page when the phone shrilled.

She dashed to answer it before it could ring again, disturbing Mikhail, and she wasn't surprised to find her editor on the other end. Derek Kent talked a lot about giving his reporters free rein and trusting them to function on their own, but in fact he liked to be kept constantly up to date on the progress of any assignment.

"Is he there?" Derek demanded without preamble.

"He's asleep," Erin answered, just as bluntly. "Or at least he was. Couldn't you have waited until tomorrow to call?"

"Sorry, honey," Derek soothed, "but you can't blame me for being anxious. Demertov's a big story."

Bristling at the inappropriate endearment, Erin wondered silently if she would ever be able to break him of such a noxious habit. On the whole Derek treated all his reporters—both male and female— equally. He would overwork and underpay anyone dumb enough to let him get away with it. Erin didn't. She had long ago demanded fair assignments and decent pay. In the process she had earned Derek's grudging respect. But that didn't stop him from calling her by little pet names whenever he felt on the defensive.

"Right now," Erin said tightly, "he's a very tired, dazed man who needs some time to get used to what's happened without anyone putting more pressure on him."

Derek laughed mockingly. "I might have known the soulful, highbrow type would bring out your protective urges. Just don't get carried away. While you're mothering the great man, keep in mind that you're supposed to be putting together a personal interview to top off your coverage. Got it?"

"Got it," Erin repeated, too amused by his description of Mikhail to take offense at his highhandedness. The thought of what would happen when the two men met made her grin. Though she and Derek had never dated, she knew that her editor was interested in her in more than a strictly professional sense. Now that he had finally secured his second divorce, she sensed he was getting ready to make a move.

Discovering that an intensely virile, commanding man had taken up residence in her apartment—at his own urging—was going to have Derek chewing his nails.

With rare submissiveness that must have left him thoroughly puzzled, Erin promised that he had nothing to worry about. She would complete the assignment to his absolute satisfaction. Still smiling, she hung up, enjoying the image of her big, self-assured editor frowning in bewilderment. Nothing in Derek's experience as a pro football star or in his successful transition to the top ranks of journalism could have prepared him for her sudden amicability.

Convinced that their conversation had gone as well as possible, for her at least, Erin switched off the living room lights and checked once more to make sure the apartment door was secure before turning in.

Her room was just across the hall from Mikhail's. She stopped for a moment, listening for any sound that might indicate he was awake, but there was none. Pleased, she closed her door and prepared for bed.

A warm shower helped her to relax enough to realize that she was more tired than she had thought. Her worry over the last few days about whether or not Mikhail would actually be released had taken its toll. She delayed only long enough to take down her gleaming auburn hair and slip on a sea-green night-gown before dropping into bed.

But once there sleep eluded her. She lay awake, staring at the ceiling. Her discontent puzzled her until she realized that for the first time in years she felt lonely. Mikhail's arrival had somehow made her uncomfortable with the solitude that she had more often than not considered essential to her well-being.

It wasn't that she shunned company. During the day she was constantly surrounded by people. Depending on her work schedule and mood, she enjoyed socializing. Three or four men she knew made pleasant escorts, in part because they accepted her insistence on casual, friendly relationships that didn't demand more of her than she was willing to give. All the passion of her warm, generous nature went into her work, a fact that was at least partially responsible for her success.

Sometimes she worried over the lack of a deep, loving commitment in her life. But never before had she lain awake dwelling on it. Turning over restlessly, she punched her pillow into a more comfortable shape and closed her eyes determinedly.

Less than an hour later she emerged from the depths of sleep wondering hazily what had awakened her. The answer wasn't long in coming. Erin sat bolt upright as a tortured scream ripped the air.

She was out of bed in an instant, flinging open first her door and then Mikhail's. Moonlight flooded his room, illuminating the man caught in the throes of some unimaginable nightmare.

Low moans broke from him, punctuated by harsh snatches of words in his own language. His big, hard body twisted helplessly on the bed as he fought to free himself from whatever horror filled his mind.

Erin reached out to him instinctively. Without pausing to think, knowing only that she had to stop his pain, she knelt beside him. As she stroked his golden hair she drew him closer. "Mikhail, wake up! You're having a nightmare. Wake up!"

Rough hands grasped her. Even though he was asleep, his strength was formidable. Before she could begin to resist he had drawn her onto the bed, pressing her slender body into the mattress and trapping her flailing arms above her head.

*"Mikhail! Don't! It's Erin!"* Fear darted through her as she felt for the first time the full impact of his weight and power. He was unconscious, tormented and liable to do anything. Fighting now in earnest,

Erin tried desperately to get free, but succeeded only in bruising herself.

Her breath was coming in low gasps that turned to a startled yelp as she realized abruptly that Mikhail was nude, and that some awareness of her womanly softness must have penetrated even his tortured sleep, because he was becoming unmistakably aroused.

In her frantic efforts to get away the thin silk of her nightgown had twisted up around her thighs. The hair-roughened length of his leg rasped against her smoothness as he shifted to hold her even closer. Still restraining both her arms in his massive grip, he slid one hand down to cup her breast.

In the shadowy light of the bedroom Erin could make out his features looming above her. His slightly uptilted gray eyes and high cheekbones gave him the look of a blond Mongol warrior. A pulse beat in his firm jaw, and his mouth was drawn in a grim, determined line that not even his silken beard could hide. The thick hair of his chest brushed against her as the corded muscles of his broad shoulders tensed. The warm, musky scent of him filled her breath.

He was the epitome of a rampaging male who had snapped the bonds of civilization and was intent only on satisfying his most primitive desires. Erin should have felt nothing but terror. Yet as his callused fingers stroked her breast through the fragile nightgown, bringing the nipple achingly alive, a fierce dart of pleasure stabbed through her.

Appalled at her responsiveness, she moaned softly. That tiny, desperate sound reached Mikhail as nothing else had been able to. For just a moment his eyes focused on her terrified features.

"Erin! My God! I'm sorry. . . ." He moved far enough away to enable her to slip a leg out from under him. But before he could fully free her, exhaustion claimed him once again, and he slumped unconscious over her body.

Trapped by his sheer size and weight, Erin had no choice but to remain where she was. She managed to wiggle into a slightly more comfortable position, only to find that her movement encouraged him to draw her even more closely against his hair-roughened torso.

Snuggled into his warmth, she gave up her efforts to put some distance between them. With a soft sigh Erin drifted off to sleep, oddly comforted by Mikhail's now gentle embrace.

That comfort lasted until just after sunrise, when she slowly became aware of someone staring at her. So intense was the scrutiny that it reached her even through the mist of her dreams. She stirred uneasily, coming awake to find Mikhail, propped up on one elbow, looking down at her.

The furious passion she had glimpsed the night before was gone. In its place was a cutting cynicism that made her wince. Mikhail caught the motion. His face hardened derisively. "Is this part of the usual hospitality?"

Erin stared at him blankly for a moment before the meaning of his words reached her. Then she blushed furiously. "How dare you! You think I'm here because . . . ?" She broke off, her face reddening even more as she followed his scathing gaze down her scantily clad body. The covers had slipped back, revealing the beauty of high, firm breasts whose contours were clearly visible through the delicate sea-green silk.

Mikhail shrugged dismissively. "Why the pretended outrage? We're both adults." His eyes were cold as he added, "I only hope you weren't disappointed. Don't take it personally, but frankly, I can't remember a thing."

Despite his callous advice, Erin took it very personally indeed. Straightening, she dragged the covers up to her shoulders and glared at him. "You admit you can't remember what happened, but you're still willing to believe I came in here on my own and crawled into bed with you to . . ."

". . . to have sex," Mikhail finished for her. Heedless of his nudity, he sat up, running a hand through his rumpled hair. "Don't misunderstand me. You're a beautiful woman. I'm happy to oblige, even though I would have preferred to be fully conscious."

"You're unbelievable!" Erin gasped. "Whatever else has happened to you, your ego is in perfect shape! I've never met a more arrogant, presumptious man! You're an absolute b—"

"That's enough!" Hard fingers dug into her shoulders as Mikhail shook her angrily. "I can appreciate a wanton in my bed, but not a fishwife!"

Staring at him in dumb amazement, Erin was unaware of how lovely and vulnerable she looked. Her long, glistening hair was in disarray, the auburn curls tumbling past her fine-boned shoulders. Her lips, bitten in her fury, pouted softly. Outrage lent a luminous glow to her skin and eyes that, under other circumstances, might have been mistaken for sensual satisfaction.

"I cannot understand how you manage to look so unsullied when you're willing to sleep with a man you hardly know," Mikhail groaned. He turned away suddenly, as though unable to bear the sight of her.

Part of Erin was tempted to take advantage of his withdrawal to escape, but her pride wouldn't let him get away with his unfounded accusations. Clutching the blanket in one hand, she indignantly raised the other. "Take a look, Mikhail. Is that what a *willing* woman has to show for a night in bed with you?"

Reluctantly, he focused his gaze on her wrist. As Erin watched, all the color drained from his face. Beneath his beard and rugged tan he turned a sickly gray. The faint bruises he had left on her pale skin stunned him.

His unmistakable distress made Erin ashamed of her own hasty action. Granted, he had behaved abominably, but allowances had to be made for his recent experiences. How had she so quickly forgotten the horror he had just passed through and that still haunted his dreams?

"The truth is," she began gently, "I bruise rather

easily. When I came in here last night you were having a nightmare. You had cried out in your sleep. I tried to wake you, but couldn't. You . . . pulled me onto the bed with you. Then you seemed to settle down, though you wouldn't let me go. I didn't want to disturb you further, so I just stayed here."

Sensing that he didn't fully believe her, she added, "Nothing else happened, Mikhail. You've been through a terrible experience. It's natural that there will be some aftereffects. So let's just forget it and—"

"You do not need to make excuses for me," he broke in huskily. "I can see that I hurt you. An apology is utterly inadequate, but please believe me, I am very sorry. Not only for last night, but for what I said to you just now." Wearily, he shook himself. "I don't understand how I could have acted so basely. It is not like me to do such a thing."

Erin swallowed hard. His profound remorse made her want to reach out and comfort him, but she sensed he would allow no such reassurance. Everything she knew about him from his writings indicated he was a man of rare decency and honor. The glimpse of raw pain she saw in his eyes made her understand how intensely he despised his own actions.

Sensitive to his need to be alone for a while to come to terms with what had happened, Erin slipped from the bed. She left the room quietly, looking back for just a moment at the man who refused to meet her gaze.

After a quick shower she dressed in warm corduroy slacks and a russet wool sweater. Leaving her hair down and dispensing with all but a minimum of makeup, she went out to the kitchen to start breakfast.

Mikhail had still not appeared when she slid the bacon onto a paper towel to drain and stuck four English muffins in the toaster. She heard the shower running in the guest bathroom, then muted sounds as he dressed.

He joined her in the kitchen just as she set the eggs out to scramble. Wearing jeans and a soft blue flannel shirt, he looked even bigger and more uncompromisingly male than he had the day before. But it wasn't his clothes that froze Erin's attention. His beard was gone. The square line of his jaw emphasized the strong, clean ruggedness of his features. With his face now fully bared to her, Erin could see just how much the events of the morning were affecting him. He was at once acutely regretful and strongly determined.

Compelled by some impulse she didn't fully understand, she spoke quickly. "Breakfast is almost ready. Would you like some coffee?"

Mikhail shook his head gravely. "No, thank you. I think it would be better if I left right away."

The whisk Erin was holding almost dropped from her fingers. "L-left?"

He moved away from the door slowly, his movements guarded, as though he were concerned he might frighten her. "We both know what almost happened last night, Erin. You can't believe that I would continue to subject you to such a threat."

He looked away from her, his eyes focusing on something she couldn't see. "It honestly never occured to me that I might be a danger to you. Even when we met at the airport, and I realized at once that I found you very attractive, I didn't stop to think that there was any reason to be concerned. But it seems that I underestimated the effects of the last year on me. It now appears that I'm all too likely to commit the very kinds of acts I have always despised."

"No!" Erin blurted, unable to bear the torment she saw as this proud, honorable man was confronted by a side of himself he had never before suspected. "You're blowing this completely out of proportion. Please, couldn't you just sit down and let us talk about it sensibly?"

Mikhail hesitated. "I'm not sure there is anything more to say. This is your home. You have every right to be safe here."

Determinedly, Erin pulled out a chair and urged him into it. She didn't fully understand how what had begun as a purely professional relationship had turned so abruptly personal, but that didn't matter. She had to stop him. "And I have every right to speak my mind about something that concerns us both. If you don't want to talk, fine. But at least do me the courtesy of listening."

A frown creased his broad forehead. For a long moment she thought he was going to refuse. When he finally lowered himself into the chair, she smiled in relief.

"As long as we're going to talk, you might as well eat, too." She bustled over to the counter, where she quickly put his breakfast on a plate, then brought it back to him. Mikhail looked at the food doubtfully, but didn't refuse it.

As he ate, Erin spoke quietly but firmly. "Last night I came to you when you were in the midst of a nightmare. I won't ask you to tell me what you were dreaming about, because I suspect that I couldn't bear to hear it. But I have enough knowledge of what you've suffered to understand how you might be driven to do something absolutely foreign to your nature."

Sitting across from him, she compelled his smoky gray gaze to meet her own. "I admit to having been frightened and to having a few bruises. But that's all. You stopped before doing anything irreparable. Despite the nightmare, despite everything that must have been in your mind at that moment, you stopped. On your own. I couldn't have prevented you from doing anything you chose. But all you did was hold me gently while we both slept. Where, then, is this great danger that you think I should fear?"

A long silence stretched out between them before Mikhail said huskily, "You are too forgiving. What about the things I said to you this morning?"

"What about them? You say you find me attractive, but I gather you prefer to be the one doing the pursuing rather than the other way around. So my presence took you by surprise and put you on the defensive. There's nothing unforgivable about that."

A rueful grin curved his sensuous mouth. "I can see now why you are such a good writer. You have an instinctive understanding of people that is enviable."

The compliment caught Erin by surprise, but she was getting used to blushing around him and hardly noticed that she did so yet again. "You should talk. Everything I've read of yours speaks of an immense sensitivity to human motivations and need. Can't you extend that same sympathy to yourself?"

"Are you quite certain," Mikhail drawled, "that you aren't with the State Department? You argue as well as any diplomat."

Uncertain how to take that, Erin stared at him worriedly. "I'm not trying to trick you, Mikhail. I just want you to stay, and I think you want that too."

Not until she said the words did Erin know how much she meant them. The thought that Mikhail would walk out of her home and her life brought a hard knot to her throat. Somehow this man whom she had met less than a day before was already very important to her. She wanted to be near him, to be warmed by his strength and gentleness. And she wanted to share herself with him, to do everything she could to make up in some small measure for his suffering and to help ease his transition into a completely new world.

But already she knew enough about Mikhail to

understand that he would not be swayed by anyone. He couldn't have survived so long under such terrible conditions without possessing an extraordinary degree of self-will and discipline. Only he could make the decision whether to go or stay.

Toying nervously with her coffee cup, Erin waited for his verdict.

# Chapter Three

"Are you absolutely certain," Mikhail asked slowly, "that you will not feel threatened in any way by me?"

Erin hesitated. In all honesty she couldn't deny being somewhat wary of him—but not for the reasons he meant. Mikhail set off yearnings within her that she had successfully repressed through all the years of her steady climb to the top of her profession. He made her aware of feelings and needs that, to say the least, confused her greatly.

Yet none of that was what he was concerned about. He had no inkling of the dizzying waves of pleasure that had washed over her when he had held her trapped in his bed. Nor did he apparently remember the traitorous response of her body that had longed to know his in the most intimate way possible. For both his sake and hers, Erin couldn't bring herself to give him any hint of the real reason why she remained concerned about what would happen if they both continued living in the same apartment.

She felt only the tiniest bit guilty as she said, "I'm sure you don't mean me any harm, Mikhail, and I think that, despite everything you've been through, you're not going to lose control of yourself and hurt me unintentionally. So I see no reason for you not to stay here."

Her answer seemed to satisfy him. He considered the situation for a while longer before at last inclining his head gravely. "Thank you, Erin. I will do everything in my power to be worthy of your trust."

A sigh of relief escaped her. Giving him a smile more dazzling than she could have suspected, she said, "I appreciate that, Mikhail. Now, suppose we give some thought to what you'd like to do today."

The warm look he sent her had its own effect, leaving Erin feeling as though the rest of the world were somehow fading away until there was no one but the two of them left. She was caught up in the sheer impact of his presence, whirling down a sun-washed path to an end she couldn't see.

Wrenching her gaze away, she forced herself to concentrate on the gray, drab landscape whose bareness never failed to dampen her spirits, only to discover that she might have been gazing at the soft green beginnings of spring for all the effect it had on her rather giddy mood. Not even the sight of stray bits of newspaper dancing up the avenue on sturdy gusts of wind could dent her happiness.

Despite the fact that the analytical part of her mind told her she was being absurdly silly, she couldn't resist the urge to indulge herself at least a little. While Mikhail was with her, she refused to let anything dim the pleasure she found in his company.

As though he too were slightly dazed by what was happening between them, Mikhail murmured, "It doesn't look like a very good day for sight-seeing, so perhaps you wouldn't mind helping me with a few errands I need to run?"

Erin agreed without even asking what he had in mind. Half an hour later she and Mikhail were finished tidying up the kitchen. He had insisted on helping, despite her assurances that she could manage alone.

"You must not think of me as a guest," he had informed her with an engaging smile. "But rather as a . . . what is the word? *Roommate?*"

Why not? That might be the safest way to handle the situation. It certainly wasn't unheard of for men and women with purely platonic relationships to share apartments. But then, very little was unheard of in New York.

She closed her eyes for a moment, thinking of what her folks back in Wyoming would say about such an arrangement before firmly putting that concern out of her mind. Her parents were both sensible, level-headed people who trusted her to make her own decisions and live by the standards they had instilled in her. She had no doubt that they would understand perfectly about Mikhail, but she none-theless couldn't help but be grateful that there was no reason for them to ever find out.

As she was getting into her warm winter coat Erin stopped, realizing that Mikhail had donned only the same thin jacket he had worn the evening before.

He caught her look of dismay and laughed gently. "Don't worry about me. I'm used to the cold."

Erin flinched, all too aware of exactly how accus-tomed he must be. In a prison camp near the Arctic Circle cold was a constant, relentless enemy. As strong and determined as he was, he must have fought a desperate battle against it every day of the past year.

Seeing her expression, Mikhail was instantly con-trite. He had spoken without thinking, never consid-ering the images he would unlock in her fertile mind. He had just told her that he wouldn't hurt her, and already he had done so.

"I am sorry, Erin," he said softly, raising a hand to her ashen cheek. "You must not let your tender heart be upset so easily. Remember, I am a free man now, largely because of your efforts. I do not intend to let the past torment me when I would do much better to concentrate on the present and future. Nor should you allow it to cause you pain."

She nodded mutely, struck as much by his under-standing as by the gentleness of his touch. With an effort she managed to smile. "Still, I think some additions to your wardrobe would be a good idea. Did they tell you in Paris that the State Department has provided funds to help get you resettled?"

Praying that he wouldn't be stubborn about accepting the money, Erin was surprised when he merely shrugged dismissively. "That won't be necessary. I already have a bank account here that should be adequate to cover my needs."

Sensing his need to be outside, where he could revel in the reality of his freedom, she accepted his suggestion that they walk instead of taking a cab.

As they strolled down Central Park she pointed out the more interesting buildings dotting the skyline. The day was overcast, but they could still make out the graceful stone residences that clustered around the Park, which gave way only grudgingly to the glass and steel towers of Midtown.

After exiting the park near Fifth Avenue, they walked along looking in the windows of the exclusive shops that crowded both sides of the street. Mikhail was fascinated by F.A.O. Schwartz, possibly the most elaborate and expensive toy shop in the world. He stared in amazement at a reproduction of an Alpine village, complete with a working railroad and ski lift. Above it, perched in a corner of the window, loomed a life-size baby giraffe carrying a multitude of other stuffed animals on its back. More teddy bears, koalas, rabbits and the like rode in a scale model of a sportscar that included a working engine, headlights and a CB radio.

"Do people actually buy such things for their children?" he asked.

"Apparently, but I suspect a lot of the toys sold here end up being enjoyed by grown-ups."

"You might be right. I seem to remember that

when I was little I always had more fun with the boxes than the actual presents."

Erin glanced up at him, startled. She supposed she really shouldn't be surprised that a man who came from such a different background could have memories very similar to her own. But knowing that he did brought him a little closer to her in a way she couldn't help but appreciate.

After continuing on down Fifth Avenue for more than ten blocks, they turned east toward Madison and the relentlessly elegant bastion of male fashion known as Brooks Brothers. Erin had visited the store several times to buy presents for her father and brothers, but she had never before ventured above the first floor. As she and Mikhail exited the elevator she glanced around curiously.

There was an air of old-world grandeur about the polished wood tables and counters, the gleaming brass drawer handles and railings, the subtle scents of fine wool and linen. Even the salesmen, scattered unobtrusively about, bespoke an earlier, more graceful era. Despite his rough dress and somewhat uncouth appearance, Mikhail was approached by an older gentleman who politely inquired if he might be of any assistance.

Erin had to stifle a laugh as she remembered that an eccentric appearance often went hand in hand with great wealth. At least, they apparently thought so at Brooks Brothers, because the kindly man did not hesitate to direct Mikhail to the finest and, not coincidentally, the most expensive suits, as well as an assortment of casual clothes, ranging from a down-filled parka to sweaters, shirts and slacks.

She barely glanced at one of the discreet price tags before clamping her mouth down hard on a gasp of dismay. Trying to catch Mikhail's eye, she was astounded when he merely nodded and said, "I presume you can begin on the order today?"

"Certainly, sir. The tailor will be happy to take your measurements, if you will just come this way."

"Do you mind waiting a few minutes?" Mikhail asked her courteously.

"No, of course not, but . . ."

She never got a chance to finish. He merely nodded his thanks and disappeared after the salesman into the fitting rooms, leaving her to wonder if she had imagined the gleam of amusement in his silvery eyes.

Before she had a chance to become bored he was back, having concluded his business with the tailor. His conversation with the salesman, who kept jotting down items in a little notebook, indicated that he was purchasing everything he needed for a complete wardrobe.

Erin wondered dazedly if he had any idea how much he was spending. She needn't have worried. Not even Brooks Brothers was so discreet as to leave the matter of payment in doubt. When Mikhail produced a store credit card to pay for his purchases, her astonishment was complete.

Helpless to stop herself, she said, "I didn't realize it was possible to get those in your homeland."

Mikhail laughed. "It isn't. The Communist state is regrettably unenlightened about such matters. This and a number of similar essentials for life in the West were waiting for me in Paris, courtesy of an old friend who knows that my childhood left me with a very unsocialistic weakness for good living."

The old friend, whoever he—or she—happened to be, might have applied for the card, but it was in Mikhail's name, forcing Erin to rapidly reassess his financial status. That, at least, was one problem she didn't have to worry about. Somehow he was in possession of more than enough money to support what even she had to admit were his luxurious tastes.

As they left the store Erin felt driven to bring up a delicate subject. Tentatively she said, "Uh . . . Mikhail . . . I don't mean to pry, but if you're carrying a large amount of cash, you should know it isn't a good idea in this city. I mean, we have something of a crime problem."

"Oh, yes, so I have heard," he said lightly. "All the time the newspapers in my country run articles about your terrible crime rates, riots, poverty, social upheaval, that sort of thing. Why, if I didn't know better from my travels in the West when I was a teenager, I would have stepped off the plane last night expecting to be bashed over the head and stripped of all my worldly possessions, such as they were."

Though she knew he was teasing her, Erin tried to remain serious. "Even so, you really do have to be careful. . . ."

His steady gray eyes met hers intently. "Do you

really think I have any cause to be afraid of your city and its people?"

Meeting his gaze, she realized what he meant. Mikhail was perfectly capable of taking care of himself in any situation. His instincts and reflexes had been toughened in the harshest circumstances. When it came to self-preservation, he was an expert. For a fleeting moment Erin actually felt sorry for any would-be mugger stupid enough to try to attack him.

"No . . . I guess you don't. . . ."

"Good; however, just in case you continue to worry, I have also availed myself of a fine old institution: traveler's checks." An engaging grin slashed across his rugged features. "So you see, I am becoming rapidly Westernized. Why, in a few more months I will undoubtedly be a full-fledged capitalist lackey. Don't you think?"

"I think," Erin giggled, "that you have a wicked sense of humor. When you were little, didn't you have any sisters to tease?"

"Unfortunately not. I was an only child. What about you?"

"I have three older brothers, but there's a big difference in our ages, so in a way I was brought up on my own. Not that I minded. There was always plenty to do back in Wyoming."

"This 'Wyoming'—it's one of the states, yes?"

"That's the place. My folks own a ranch there."

Mikhail's eyes widened slightly. "A ranch? You mean with cowboys and broncos and things like that?"

"Well, no, not exactly. . . ." Seeing his disappointment, she relented hastily. "I guess you could describe it that way. My father runs cattle and raises horses. He does a little planting on the side, but mostly his business is in livestock."

"Ah, now that is the life! A little piece of land, crops ripening in the sun, a few cows fattening in the fields."

"Uh . . . there aren't really many small farms left in this country. Mom and Dad's place is about five thousand acres."

Mikhail appeared to be truly stunned. He shook his head in amazement. "They own all that themselves?"

"Them and the bank. Even though Dad has borrowed a lot less money than some other ranchers, he grumbles about the interest rates."

"But it is still his land?"

"Very much so. It's been in our family for three generations, ever since my great-grandfather, Sean Hennessey, trekked west with one of the wagon trains and staked it out for himself."

"I have heard of such things," Mikhail murmured, "but I never actually met someone who lived in such a place. How did you bring yourself to leave?"

"I ask myself that, too, sometimes," Erin admitted. "I guess I just wanted to see more of the world, and then . . ." She hesitated, surprised at how close she had come to something she had never talked about before.

"Then . . . what?" Mikhail prodded gently. They had stopped at a street corner. The wind whistled along the caverns of steel and glass buildings, some sporting brave holiday decorations that looked stark and unappealing without the cloak of darkness. People hurried by, their bodies hunched against the cold. From far off in the distance Erin could hear the signal horns of the boats plying the rivers. One of the more evocative names for New York flashed through her mind: Oz on the Hudson. It was that, and more. But she didn't regret the steps that had led her down the yellow brick road, even though some had been more painful than others.

"My brothers will inherit the ranch," she said softly. "That's only fair, since they're the ones with both the interest and skills to keep it going. If I had stayed I'd naturally have wanted a home of my own. And to get that I'd probably have ended up married to some local boy."

"And you didn't wish such a marriage?"

"It wasn't a question of not wishing. . . . There was someone I would have liked to marry, but he . . . he preferred a cousin of mine."

She paused, expecting the usual platitudes that she'd heard all too often before. But Mikhail voiced none of them. Instead he asked, "Are they happy together?"

"Yes . . . I think so. They certainly seem happy." She smiled faintly. "Last time I was home Katie was expecting her third child. She was hoping for a girl, but it turned out to be another boy. Not that she minded, of course."

"Then, if this man you wanted is happy with your cousin, it's fortunate he did not marry you instead. He would have made you miserable."

"I wouldn't have done him any good, either." Erin laughed, surprised that she could do so. It was the first time she had ever joked about the fact that Frank hadn't loved her. "I think even then I had my heart set on seeing the world."

"And have you?" Mikhail asked, picking up on her lighter mood. He took her arm as they crossed the street and continued to hold it tucked against him as they strolled up Fifth Avenue.

"A fair portion of it. What about you? I remember reading that your father was a diplomat and that you grew up in several of the major European capitals."

"That's right. My father's rank was sufficient to allow him to bring his family with him. I lived in Paris, London and Rome while I was still very young. His last posting was in Washington, but we weren't there long enough for me to see much of your country."

"What happened to him?" Erin asked softly. She already knew part of the answer, but as was so often the case in such matters, there were big chunks missing.

"He was purged," Mikhail said matter-of-factly. "During the early 1960s there was a great deal of turmoil in my country, mostly behind the scenes. Many men lost their positions because they were no longer considered trustworthy. That was especially true with those who had lived in the West. Their loyalty was automatically suspect."

"Is your father still alive?"

"No, he died in a labor camp years ago. I'm not sure exactly when, because by that time I was also on the run from the authorities."

"And your mother . . . ?"

Mikhail's eyes hardened. All the life and warmth abruptly vanished from them. "She remarried a party official who could support her in the fashion to which she had become accustomed. The last I heard, she was telling people she had never been married before or had any children."

Erin couldn't hide the sympathy that she knew was written clearly on her face. When she contrasted such behavior with that of her own loving family . . .

"Do not pity me," Mikhail ordered harshly.

"I d-don't. . . ."

"Then what was that look I just saw? No, Erin, if you must pity anyone, let it be my mother. She sold herself no differently from the way any whore would."

"You shouldn't talk about your mother like that."

"Why not? I have only said the truth." His expression made it clear that far more determined people than she had tried—unsuccessfully—to stop him from speaking his mind.

Disheartened, Erin was silent as they walked several more blocks. They were nearing the majestic granite facade of St. Patrick's Cathedral when Mikhail suddenly sighed. "It's a good thing there weren't more people around to hear me say that. Some spokesman for the oppressed! I sounded like a hurt little boy."

"You sounded like a man who has suffered a great deal," Erin corrected gently.

"As I believe I have already commented, you are very understanding."

"No more so than you. . . ." Catching herself, Erin laughed. "We could stand here all day and trade compliments, but it *is* a bit nippy. What do you say we go home and find out what's left in the refrigerator."

"I will gladly agree with the first part, but not the second. It's my turn to cook, so first we must stop off at a food store."

"Your turn? But you don't have to . . ."

"Isn't it only proper for good roommates to share the chores?"

"Well, yes, but . . ."

"But what? Ah, I see what is troubling you. You don't think I can cook. I will have you know, Miss Hennessey, that such lack of faith wounds me deeply. Admittedly it has been some time since I have—how do you say—slung hash? But I can still find my way around a kitchen."

"You may not have spent much time in Washington, but you sure picked up your share of Americanisms. Okay, you win. We'll go food shopping."

The shop they chose was Zabar's, the gourmet delicatessen that was famous throughout New York and beyond. "I have heard of this place," Mikhail said as he looked around in fascination at the crowd of shoppers crammed between counters of cold cuts, cheeses, smoked fish, breads, pastries, coffees and every other manner of delicacy the mind of man had managed to dream up. "But I wouldn't have believed the stories if I hadn't actually been here. This is as far from any store in my country as it's humanly possible to get."

"Zabar's doesn't have much in common with other stores anywhere," Erin said dryly. "I would be willing to bet it's one of the few places in the world that's genuinely in a class by itself."

Despite the mass of people they had no difficulty getting waited on at any of the various counters. Erin listened silently as Mikhail debated the merit of various kinds of salmon with the knowledgeable deli man, selected herbs with the help of a little old lady swathed in black, who, it turned out, came from a village near his own hometown, and examined half-a-dozen types of coffee under the indulgent eye of a young lady who seemed willing to wait all afternoon for him to make his selection. Back outside, their arms laden with packages, they hailed a taxi and headed for Erin's apartment. Once there, Mikhail took charge.

Rolling up his sleeves, he frowned at the combination microwave and convection oven before dismissively pushing the food processor off to one side. Under his patient direction Erin spent the next hour peeling, chopping and pounding as they concocted dishes she had never had but that, with each passing moment, began to smell more and more appetizing. The kitchen was filled with delectable aromas when she excused herself long enough to tidy her hair and slip into a fresh sweater, the one she had been wearing having acquired a decided scent of onions, paprika and sour cream.

Mikhail had promised her a sampling of all his favorite dishes, and he didn't disappoint. They started off with *kulebiaka*, light pastries stuffed with mushrooms and salmon, followed by a delectable chicken dish flavored with nutmeg, paprika and cognac, potatoes stuffed with caviar, and finally, for dessert, a *pasha* of cheese, sugar, candied fruits and almonds, washed down by the strong coffee that h admitted was the only non-traditional element of the dinner, but which he had missed far too much to do without.

Relaxed and replete, they settled in front of the living-room fireplace after sharing the tidying up chores. Erin had tried to convince him to let her take care of them alone, since he had done most of the cooking, but once again Mikhail had insisted.

Erin had given in bemusedly. She still had trouble believing that she was sharing her apartment with a tender giant of a man whose remarkable courage and spirit drew her as potently as his compellingly masculine strength and virility. It was a heady combination that sent her senses reeling. For the first time in her life she was becoming truly aware of her full potential as a woman. Mikhail's nearness alone was enough to wake forces within her that frightened even as they excited.

Settled in front of the fire with snifters of brandy, neither felt any need to speak. As the wind picked up outside droplets of snow splattered against the windows. But inside all was warm and secure. In the aftermath of a delicious meal, with a cheerful blaze holding the darkness at bay, they were more than content to simply enjoy each other's company.

Seated close together on the couch, they began to talk quietly of little things, small details of their lives, deliberately avoiding the vast issues that had brought them together. By tacit agreement they didn't speak of the concerns facing an expatriate writer and a journalist dedicated to helping him spread his message of freedom and hope. Instead they indulged some measure of the need they felt to learn about each other purely as a man and a woman.

Erin laughed as Mikhail described his childhood misadventures in the embassies to which his father had been posted. "I was what you call a holy terror," he admitted unrepentently. "Being one of the few children in any of the places we lived, I tended to be rather spoiled. That and the fact that my father's rank made it impolitic for anyone to criticize me led to some pranks I blush to think of even now."

"I'll bet you weren't as badly behaved as I was," Erin claimed. "Being the only girl in the family, and the youngest child, I got into more trouble than I was worth. My poor parents despaired of my ever learning to behave myself."

A teasing gleam darkened Mikhail's silvery gaze. "And did you?"

"Oh, I finally accepted the fact that it wasn't nice to drop ice down ladies' dresses and put frogs in people's beds. But I never quite lost the urge to stir things up a bit. I guess that's why I became a reporter."

"Yes," he said softly, "I think every writer is spurred at least in part by a certain childlike enjoyment of the world, even when it is at its worst."

Erin stared up at him, fascinated by the play of the firelight against his burnished skin. Thick sun-tipped lashes hid his eyes, making it impossible for her to see his expression. But she was acutely conscious of the sensual fullness of his mouth, which softened as he studied her in turn.

His big hand moved slowly to cup the back of her head, his callused fingers tangling in the silken skeins of her auburn hair. "Erin . . . you are so beautiful . . . like an angel come to earth. . . ."

The husky timbre of his voice resonated through her, making her tremble. "I'm not . . ."

A faint smile curved the lips that were very close to her own. "Not what? Not beautiful, or not an angel?"

"N-neither. . . . I'm just a woman. . . ."

He laughed throatily. "Oh, yes . . . that you are . . . warm and gentle and giving. . . ." His head bent, and his arms drew her closer. The warmth and strength of his big body reached out to engulf her.

Despite the power she sensed within him and the desire she knew he was holding tightly in check, Erin felt no hesitation. There was only a sense of rightness, of something long wished for, as her softness yielded to the velvet steel of his embrace.

Mikhail's firm, seeking mouth tasted the smoothness of her brow, the curve of her cheek and the slender line of her throat before he at last gave in to her wordless plea and savored the sweetness of her lips.

Slowly, without the slightest sense of haste or intrusion, his tongue probed the moist secrets of her mouth, meeting hers in an erotic duel that sent coils of fire spiraling through her.

Erin moaned softly, her arms tightening around him, needing to bring him closer yet. He was so strong and gentle, so attuned to her every need and response. . . . And she wanted him with a fierce hunger that shocked her even as she welcomed it joyfully.

For the moment, at least, she refused to listen to the faint whispers of caution warning her that she was rushing into something vastly beyond her control, something that might turn out very differently from anything she could envision.

# Chapter Four

"There's a staff meeting this afternoon at three o'clock," Jenny Stewart said, "and the proofs of the article you're doing are on your desk, along with a stack of phone messages. Oh, and Mr. Kent wants to see you right away."

Erin nodded glumly. She had only been out for a couple of days and already her small office looked as though a tornado had hit it. Despite Jenny's best efforts, there was only so much the young secretary could do, especially with three other reporters to look after.

Mail, research material, drafts of pending articles, photos and all sorts of effluvia littered every available surface. Stacks of books were precariously balanced on the shelves and floor. A lone plant somehow managed to flourish in the midst of the mess, but Erin doubted that she would be able to cope as well.

Jenny smiled sympathetically. "It really isn't much worse than usual. You've just been away long enough to forget."

"The human brain blocks out scenes like this. It's part of our instinctive self-defense mechanism."

"Why don't you sit down, relax, and take a few minutes to tell me all the news?"

"What news?" Erin muttered, still faintly dazed by what she was going to have to wade through in the next few hours.

"About *him*, of course! Mikhail Demertov. He did get here, didn't he?"

A dull flush crept up Erin's cheeks. She ducked her head slightly, pretending great interest in a memo. The soft apricot wool dress she wore suddenly seemed too warm, despite the chilly day.

"Oh, sure, he got here. Everything's fine. Uh . . . didn't you say Derek wanted to see me?"

Jenny waved that aside. Her honey-blond curls practically wiggled with excitement as she demanded, "How can you be so calm about it? Mikhail Demertov! If he's anything like his books, he's positively dreamy!"

"He writes about the brutal oppression of people longing for freedom. What's *dreamy* about that?"

"The way he does it, of course. He's so . . . sensitive and . . . deep."

A soft sigh escaped Erin. She supposed comments like that were inevitable from a nineteen-year-old, even one as sensible as Jenny. But they were still a little hard to take first thing in the morning. Trying to persuade herself that her reluctance to talk about Mikhail had nothing to do with what had happened between them the previous night, she said, "I'll tell him you said so, but right now I think I'd better see what Derek wants."

Jenny's china blue eyes darkened. With one of those remarkable shifts from silliness to maturity that occured at her age, she said, "Erin, is anything wrong? I mean . . . you seem sort of upset. . . ."

Embarrassed at not being able to hide her feelings more successfully, Erin shook her head. "No, I'm fine. . . . I didn't mean to sound so abrupt. I have a lot on my mind, but that's no excuse." Smiling slightly, she added, "I'm sure Mikhail will be coming by here eventually. If you like, I'll introduce you."

"*Like?* I'd love it. But . . . you won't really tell him I said he was dreamy, will you?"

"No, of course not. Although—" her smile broadened as her usual good humor began to assert itself "—between the two of us, he really is!"

Jenny's eyes opened wider, along with her mouth. But before she could launch into the stream of questions that comment had inspired, Erin was gone, hurrying down the corridor to the managing editor's office.

Derek Kent was behind the huge marble-topped table that served as his desk. His big linebacker's body was comfortably ensconced in a burnished leather chair that some of the less-reverent members of his staff claimed bore an intentional ressemblance to a throne.

His thick chestnut hair was neatly trimmed around his powerful head. A stray lock fell across his broad forehead, above coal-black eyes that had long ago mastered the art of the intimidating look. As usual his suit jacket was hung over the back of the chair, his shirt sleeves were rolled up to his bare sinewy forearms and his tie was undone to reveal the tanned column of his throat.

At forty-two Derek Kent was a man long accustomed to getting exactly what he wanted in both his business and private lives. He was intelligent, clever, determined and not overly burdened by scruples. Men took to him instantly, enjoying the virile sense of camaraderie he exuded. Women needed only one look to guess that he would be a highly proficient, demanding lover. More than a few had found out they were right.

Erin regarded him warily. She wasn't at all immune to his attractions, but had no intention of ever doing anything about them. Very simply, she didn't trust Derek Kent an inch. For all the surface charm, he had a tendency to use people for his own benefit.

Winter sunlight poured in through the ceiling-high windows behind him. During other times of the year, when the sun was more intense, the glare striking anyone sitting in the visitors' chairs could be blinding. That was deliberate. Just as when he'd been a football player, Derek wasn't above taking any advantage to get what he wanted from those unfortunate enough to wander into his den.

During their first meeting, when she had been applying for the job at *Focus*, Erin had thrown him by simply getting up and moving her chair out of the sun's path. Four years later she was still convinced that simple action had won her the position. Certainly Derek had never forgotten it, as his first words when he spotted her confirmed.

"Come on in, honey. Take a seat. Sun's not in your eyes, is it?"

"I'd let you know if it were," she said, smiling sweetly. Smoothing her apricot wool skirt, she crossed her legs while ignoring his appreciative glance.

Several moments passed before he asked, "How's your house guest this morning?"

"Still asleep when I left, but I'm sure he's doing fine. He's making a remarkable adjustment."

"Oh, yeah? Tell me about it."

Sighing, Erin filled him in on the shopping expedition of the day before while omitting all the more personal details. When she finished Derek looked far more interested than he had before. "So the guy isn't hurting for bucks. That's a twist I didn't expect. Where's the money coming from?"

"I have no idea."

"Why haven't you asked?"

Good question. Normally she wouldn't have hesitated to probe every aspect of a story, but somewhere along the line she had stopped thinking about Mikhail in purely professional terms.

"It's too soon," she hedged. "He needs to settle in more before I start pestering him."

"I thought you said he was making a remarkable adjustment."

"He is, but why press our luck?"

Derek frowned. "This doesn't sound like you, Erin. You're always the first one out of the starting gate at the mere hint of a good story. What's going on?"

Carefully keeping her gaze locked on his so as not to give the appearance of being evasive, she said quietly, "You've got to realize we're not dealing with some reclusive pop star or uncooperative politician. This man just spent the last year in a place that can probably be best described as hell on earth. Before that he was on the run, constantly hunted and never knowing when he'd be betrayed. Now all of a sudden he's free, safe and plunged into the middle of material luxury beyond anything he's known since he was a child. I know I'm repeating myself, but he needs more time before we try to get him to relive what he's been through."

Leaning back in his chair, Derek folded both arms behind his head and sneered. *"Intellectuals.* They're all the same. Sensitive, tortured souls who have to be protected and coddled. They wouldn't last ten seconds out on the football field."

"And how long would you have lasted in that prison camp where Mikhail was held?" Erin snapped. For once she had run out of patience with her boss's macho bias. "Your survival skills may be fine on a hundred yards of Astroturf and in the corporate jungle, but believe it or not, there are more demanding arenas. I've just spent the weekend with a man who survived what most of us can't even imagine. If you're as smart as you like to think, you'll take my advice and give him room to breathe. Otherwise you're liable to find yourself up against a brand of toughness you never even knew existed."

Long, strained moments of silence followed her pronouncement. A pulse began to beat in Derek's square jaw. He had made a career of never being outclassed by anyone and wasn't about to change that.

Irately he growled, "What lit your fire, lady? Or do I have to ask? Sounds like it didn't take this guy very long to get to you. Of course, after all those months up near the Arctic, I guess he wouldn't be turned off by the threat of a little frostbite."

"Is that little innuendo supposed to upset me?" Erin shot back. "Nothing you say changes the fact that I can only cover this story my way. And that means not pushing him."

Implicit in her words was the suggestion that Mikhail wasn't the only one who shouldn't be pushed. Derek should know her well enough by now to realize that she didn't respond any better to that sort of treatment than he would himself.

For a moment they glared at each other stubbornly, neither wanting to be the first to give in. Finally he whistled softly. "It's a good thing I could never stand the mealy-mouthed type."

Erin almost sighed with relief, but she was still

wary enough to ask, "Does that mean I can handle the story my way?"

Derek groaned. "You don't give an inch, do you? I almost feel sorry for Demertov. The guy will never know what hit him."

Since that was as close to a vote of confidence as she was likely to get, Erin opted to overlook the implicit suggestion that she was merely setting Mikhail up for a fall. Little did Derek know, she thought glumly as they went on to chat of other things. She was the one precariously balanced on an emotional edge, and she might well have tumbled off the night before if Mikhail hadn't pulled her back.

The memory of how his kiss had made her feel was still powerful enough to send shivers of warmth radiating through her. How Derek would laugh if he knew that the woman he regarded as a formidable challenge to his masculine charms had so easily succumbed to a man she barely knew.

And yet, was that really the case? In a sense she had known Mikhail for years through his writing. Their minds and spirits had been attuned long before she'd experienced the shock of their mutual physical attraction. And that it was mutual she had no doubt. Mikhail had made it eminently clear that he desired her every bit as much as she did him. But he was also unwilling to plunge into a relationship that might end up hurting them both.

In the bright light of morning she was grateful for the conscientiousness and concern that had enabled him to gently but firmly end the passionate encounter before either was irrevocably set on a course that might lead only to pain.

"It is too soon, beautiful Erin," he had murmured shakily. "What we feel is very powerful . . . almost frighteningly so. . . . We must go carefully to make this everything it can be for both of us."

He was right, of course, but that hadn't made it any easier for her to sleep after he had left her at her bedroom door with a tenderly chaste kiss on her forehead. She suspected that he had found it every bit as hard to put the fiery passion of their bodies' responses from his mind. When she had peered into his room that morning to tell him she was leaving for the office, she had found him asleep in a tumbled bed that looked as though it had been the scene of considerable tossing and turning.

An undeniable sense of satisfaction curved her mouth as she remembered how, even in the midst of her confusion and disappointment, she had felt infinitely cared for and protected.

The smile faded when Derek suddenly interrupted her thoughts. "I'm not keeping you from something more important, am I?" His tone made it clear that absolutely nothing was more important than a meeting with her managing editor and that she would be well advised to remember that.

"Oh, no, of course not. Uh . . . it's just that I am a little concerned about Mikhail. Being on his own for the first time today and all."

"I asked you to take the guy home with you so you could interview him, not turn into a surrogate mother." Derek sighed exasperatedly. "If you want some-one to coddle, how about a harassed managing editor?"

Erin couldn't help but laugh. Even though she knew that the lost little boy look he was sending her was only one more attempt in his on-again, off-again campaign to maneuver her into seeing him on a social basis, she couldn't help but be impressed.

"I'd have to get in line," she said coolly. "Be-tween that rugged he-man attitude you usually proj-ect and the poor-little-me pout you can put on at a second's notice, you must have to beat the women off with a club." Standing up swiftly, she added, "And while you're doing that, I'll see about clearing away the mess that's accumulated on my desk."

"If you weren't such a damn good reporter . . ." Derek was muttering as she departed. His secretary, a ravishingly gorgeous blonde whom he had hired to be decorative, only to discover that she could both type up a storm and had a husband as big as Derek himself, winked as Erin passed through the outer office.

Erin had no doubt that by afternoon the grapevine would know that she had once again gone head to head with her boss and emerged unscathed. Now, if only she could continue to keep him away from Mikhail long enough to straighten out her own bewildering feelings and make some progress on the story. . . .

"How did it go?" Jenny asked as Erin passed by on her way back to her office. Jenny was almost as fascinated by their managing editor as she was by Mikhail, but fortunately that didn't get in the way of her work.

She kept right on typing as Erin said, "Okay, I guess. I don't suppose the elves shoveled off my desk while I was gone?"

"Nope, but Joe Caniglio dropped by to ask if you could cover for him on Christmas. Can you believe he drew holiday duty for the fourth time this year?"

"That's because he's the junior man on staff. But since I'll be in town anyway, I'll be glad to stay by my phone in case anything comes up. He's got several kids, doesn't he?"

Jenny nodded. "Three, all under the age of six, so you can imagine what a big deal Christmas must be at his house." She hesitated a moment before asking, "Are you really disappointed about not being able to go home to Wyoming?"

"A little, but when I explained to my folks about Mikhail suddenly being released and my wanting to be here, they understood perfectly. Of course, if I'd known what good shape he's in, I would just have invited him to go along with me."

"Couldn't you still?"

"'Fraid not. The whole Far West got hit by a huge blizzard last night. According to this morning's news they'll be socked in solid for days. Anyway, I've always wanted to see New York during Christmas, so now's my chance."

"You sure do roll with the punches," Jenny said admiringly. "If I were in your shoes I'd probably be all upset about missing the holiday with my folks, plus a nervous wreck about how to cope with Mikhail."

From the lofty position of her twenty-eight years Erin murmured, "You don't cope with men like him."

Jenny finally stopped typing. She looked up with definite interest, hoping to learn something far more useful than how to get ahead in journalism. "What do you do?"

"You . . ." Erin shrugged, shaking her head ruefully. "Darned if I know. I've never met anyone like him before."

The younger girl laughed. Her innocent blue eyes held a definitely devilish gleam as she said, "Then maybe you'd better just hang on and hope for the best. It could be a heck of a ride."

Erin had the sneaky suspicion it would be just that, but she wasn't about to say so. Back in her own office, she plunked herself down in front of her overloaded desk with every intention of putting the previous night behind her and getting on with what might well be one of the most important stories of her career.

# Chapter Five

But when she got home that evening there was no sign of her "story." The apartment was dark and quiet, the winter chill permeating even its normally cheerful corners.

Erin stood in the entry hall, glancing around apprehensively. Once again she was struck by the emptiness of the place. What had always been a warm, cheerful home suddenly seemed almost unbearably lonely.

Taking a deep breath to calm the unaccustomed racing of her heart, she called, "Mikhail . . . I'm home."

No answer. Maybe he had fallen asleep. Not bothering to take off her coat, she stuck her head in the guest room. It was empty. The bed was neatly made, and there were no stray clothes or other items left scattered about. If it weren't for the book lying open on the bedside table she might have thought she had imagined the events of the previous few days.

Where had he gone? Erin returned to the living room and paced back and forth nervously. It didn't seem likely that he would have gone out for a walk on such a gloomy afternoon, with snow threatening. But then, she really had very little idea of what he was or was not inclined to do. Perhaps, after all those months of confinement, he hadn't been able to resist the urge to get out and roam around.

That must be it, she told herself as she finally took off her coat and put her briefcase away. Fixing herself a cup of tea, she stared at the clock. It really wasn't all that late. She had no reason to be worried, especially since Mikhail was far better equipped than the vast majority of New Yorkers to handle any difficulty he might encounter.

But what about unforeseen dangers which might threaten him specifically? It wasn't impossible that his government might regret releasing him to the West. Men of his courageous and outspoken nature were a constant threat to repressive regimes. It wasn't unheard of for them to die suddenly and mysteriously.

You're being ridiculous, she told herself sternly, imagining conspiracies where there are none. Yet her doubts persisted. Had it even occurred to Mikhail that he should be especially cautious? Or was he so exuberant about his unexpected freedom that he might forget even the most basic rules for survival instilled in him over the years?

A long, trying hour passed during which her vivid imagination conjured up all sorts of distressing visions. She grew steadily more upset, despite her best efforts to reason with herself. It wasn't like her to be overly protective of anyone, much less a man she had only met a couple of days before. But then, nothing seemed to be the same since Mikhail had walked into her life.

Within the space of a few dozen hours she had come close to forgetting her deeply held conviction that physical intimacy belonged only in a relationship where there was already firm emotional commitment, and she had lost sight of her professional responsibility to get the story without regard to personal considerations. So why should she be surprised that her usually calm, rational facade was also crumbling?

Determined to distract herself, she changed into soft, well-worn jeans and a bulky mauve turtleneck that highlighted the delicate flush of her cheeks. Pulling out the pins that had held her hair in a neat chignon, she brushed it until it crackled.

She was just returning to the kitchen when she heard Mikhail letting himself in with the extra set of keys she had provided. Rushing to the door, she found him maneuvering a large and obviously heavy carton through the narrow entranceway.

A slashing smile lit his face. His gaze missed nothing of her slightly disheveled appearance. The thoroughly male gleam of appreciation made her self-conscious, but also pleased her. Their eyes met, hers drinking in the sheer size and strength of him. His golden mane of hair was touseled by the wind, which had also blown his jacket taut against his chest. His burnished skin was slightly flushed, making his silvery eyes look even more vivid by contrast.

The vigorous cold of the outdoors clung to him, but beneath it she could sense the warmth of his powerful body and sense the tensile steel that ran through him. Feeling inordinately foolish for having been so worried, she turned her attention firmly to the carton he carried.

"What's that?"

"A typewriter. I have decided it is time for me to get back to work."

As she followed him Mikhail took the box into the bedroom, opened it and pulled out an electric typewriter, which he proceeded to install on the desk near the window.

"I hope you don't mind," he said, "that I want to start writing before looking for an apartment and doing all the other things I need to get settled."

"Of course not!" Erin was genuinely appalled that such a thought would even have occured to him. "Nothing's more important than your writing. If you feel able to get back to work so soon, you shouldn't let anything distract you."

"Now, *that* may prove very difficult," he teased, caressing her with his gaze. Despite the bulky sweater and jeans, he seemed to have no trouble discerning the softly rounded body he had come so close to possessing the night before.

It amazed Erin how a single look from him could transform her back into an adolescent. More than a little flustered, she said, "W-whether it is or not, I'm delighted you want to write again. If there's any way I can help . . ."

Mikhail took a step closer, his expression suddenly gentle as he murmured, "But you already have, more than you will ever know."

"You m-mean by helping to get you out? But lots of people were involved in that. . . ."

"Not just that. Forty-eight hours ago I believed there was no beauty or warmth left in the world. I thought life had become a grim struggle stripped of all redeeming grace. Then I stepped off a plane and met you." A smile curved his hard mouth. "To say the least, you have managed to restore my faith in the essential wonder of life in a miraculously short time. And you have made me look forward to the future in a way I did not think was possible."

Deeply moved, Erin couldn't hide the effect his words had on her. She was at once immensely touched and relieved to know that he shared the belief that something extraordinary was happening between them. When his hand gently touched the curve of her cheek she made no effort to withdraw. Rather, she welcomed his touch with every fiber of her being. They came together as naturally as if they had known each other for a lifetime.

Drawn close against his body, she luxuriated in the sense of protective strength that reached out to enfold her. Her hands reached up along the hard, sinewy line of his back to stroke his broad shoulders. He was so near that she could clearly make out every shadowed plane and sculpted angle of his face. There was nothing gentle about his features. They had been carved by the harsh wind of experience. Yet his eyes were still capable of tenderness, and there was no roughness in his touch. He held her reverently, as though almost afraid she would break.

Breathing in deeply, she savored the crisp, clean scent of him. Her fingers tangled in the silken pelt of his hair as a soft moan escaped her. "Oh, Mikhail . . . please . . . I want . . ."

"So do I, sweet angel," he murmured in the instant before his mouth claimed hers.

Erin's eyes fluttered shut. Her body melted against his, no hint of resistance or doubt marring the perfection of a closeness sweeter and more profound than any she had ever known. She was vaguely aware of his powerful arms tightening around her, drawing her upward until she stood balanced on the tips of her toes. All her weight was thrown against him, but he took it easily. His big hands slipped down the slender line of her back, making her arch like a contented kitten. A low rumble of pleasure escaped him as he felt the quiver of desire that ran through her.

"Beautiful. . . ." he muttered thickly before deepening the kiss to an intensity that made all her senses sing. The silken roughness of his hair beneath her fingers contrasted vividly with the velvet smoothness of his tongue gently tasting her with slow, savoring strokes. The fresh, natural scent of him filled her even as the surging rhythm of his heart echoed her own.

No thought of protest dimmed Erin's delight as his hands slipped up under her loose sweater to stroke the petal-soft skin of her waist before reaching upward to the fullness of her breasts. When he took them gently in his big, calloused palms, a low whimper of pleasure rippled from her. Slowly, tenderly, his thumbs rubbed over her throbbing nipples as he leaned forward, holding her within the arc of his body.

Although she could feel the full intensity of his own arousal, Erin never doubted that he was in complete control of himself. Knowing that enabled her to trust him absolutely and to abandon herself to caresses that might otherwise have alarmed her.

For endless moments they stood enraptured by each other. Far below on the street the usual rush-hour traffic rumbled and honked, but they didn't hear it. The world narrowed down to a single time and place, an interlude of utterly private discovery and communication.

When they at last drew away from each other, they were both dazed and exhilarated. Erin understood more than ever why Mikhail was determined that they not rush into an intimate relationship. She needed no great experience to tell her that when they did come together in that way, forces would be unleashed that, once freed, could never again be readily contained.

"I think," Mikhail murmured shakily, "that perhaps we should go out to dinner tonight."

Erin agreed immediately. They needed to put some distance between themselves and the wide, inviting bed that beckoned so seductively.

They chose a small Spanish restaurant less than a block from the apartment, which, though comfortably casual, served only the finest quality and variety of traditional dishes. Over a Catalonian shellfish stew that included lobster, shrimp, mussels and clams, they talked as easily as longtime friends.

A warm glow of contentment enveloped them by the time Erin said, "I have a favor to ask. I really would like your help with a very important project."

"Of course," Mikhail said readily. "What is it?"

Her smile broadened. "Christmas, of course. I haven't done a thing to get ready for it, and it's only a few days away."

"Christmas. . . . In some of the cities where we lived people celebrated that. There were always a lot of decorations up in the streets and a special kind of singing. . . ." He paused, searching for the word.

"Caroling. You'll hear plenty of that this week, and the decorations are already up. I guess you were still too tired to notice them when we went shopping, but perhaps, if you'd like . . ." Breaking off, Erin looked at him uncertainly. She wasn't sure if he would share her enthusiasm.

"Perhaps what?" Mikhail encouraged gently. "Your eyes are all lit up, and for just a moment you looked as I imagine you must have when you were a little girl. Now you must finish what you were going to say so I will know what caused such an expression of happiness."

Self-consciously Erin complied. "Perhaps after we finish here you'd like to go for a walk and see all the decorations and hear the carolers. The City turns into such a magical place at Christmas that it would be a shame for you to miss it."

To her delight Mikhail agreed at once. The delicious orange caramel custard that concluded the meal prompted them to linger awhile longer, but they were soon out on the street, joining the eager crowd of strollers wandering along the avenues.

In a city aglow with a seemingly infinite sea of lights it was never truly dark, but a cloud-filled sky hovered over them like a thick, velvety blanket, against which the Christmas decorations stood out radiantly. The winter-bare branches of the trees were festooned with strands of tiny bulbs that looked like diamonds tossed into the air by a giant's hand. Every store window glittered with elaborate displays of angels and elves, wise men and reindeer. Wide-eyed children pressed their noses against the glass panes as their parents looked on, recapturing their own sense of awe at a season wrapped in magic.

Mikhail smiled down at her, clearly sharing her pleasure. Hand-in-hand they meandered along Fifth Avenue until at last they came to Rockefeller Center, where an immense Christmas tree towered above the people who had come to admire it. A group of Salvation Army carolers was singing nearby, their voices rising harmoniously to the night sky in a hymn for peace.

Catching Mikhail's puzzled look, Erin realized that he wasn't accustomed to seeing people in uniform behave in such a manner. Quietly she explained who they were and why they were standing patiently, hour after hour in the cold, to collect money for the less fortunate.

When she finished, and had made her own donation, Mikhail did the same. She had no idea how much he gave, but she guessed from the startled reaction of the young woman standing next to the kettle into which all contributions were dropped that it was substantial. She thanked him warmly, though only to the same sincere degree that she did everyone else, no matter what they gave.

As they walked forward for a closer look at the tree Mikhail suddenly asked, "It just occurred to me when you spoke of the people in the City who don't have families that you had probably planned to spend the holiday in Wyoming. Was that the case?"

"Not after I learned you were coming." Briefly Erin explained to him about her concern that he would be in much worse condition than had turned out to be the case. Teasingly she said, "If I'd known you were in such good shape, I would have figured you'd have enough stamina to cope with my family, and I'd have invited you to go out there with me. But we can't try to make the trip now because of the blizzard that hit this morning. I spent one Christmas in an airport, and I don't intend to go through that again. We'll just have to make our own holiday right here in the City."

"I don't really know what that involves," Mikhail laughed, "but it sounds delightful. Where do we start?"

"Well . . . if we really wanted to do it up right, we'd get a tree."

His gaze shifted from her glowing face to the giant fir towering above them, rising up and up until at last it ended in a blazing star at the top. "Like that one?"

"Not quite as big, but you get the idea. Then we'd have to have decorations . . . a wreath for the door . . . Christmas music . . . all the traditional foods."

She couldn't quite keep a note of wistfulness out of her voice as she visualized past holidays at the ranch. Mikhail caught the fleeting emotion she tried to suppress. Plump flakes of snow began to drift gently out of the sky, glistening against her hair and lashes. Gently he put an arm around her shoulders and drew her more closely against the shelter of his body.

"Then we'd better get started right away, sweet angel," he teased. "It sounds as though we have a busy night ahead!"

Outside a delicatessen near the apartment they found a six-foot-tall fir tree that Erin tried to tell herself was too big, but which Mikhail rightly surmised she longed for and insisted on buying. Further down the street, at a tiny shop about to close for the evening, they selected lights, ornaments and several records of Christmas music.

After they staggered home under their burdens,

Erin left Mikhail to get the tree up in its bright-red stand while she ran out to raid the nearest food store. She got back to find Handel's *Messiah* on the stereo, a fragrant log blazing away in the fireplace, and the fir already partially strung with lights.

Pausing at the door, she took in the scene as a warm sense of contentment stole over her. The feeling was similar to what she had always experienced at her parents' home, and yet different. Along with delight in the pleasures and sentiments of the holiday, she felt a deeply rooted sense of satisfaction in the fact that she was able to help create such a magical time and share it with another person.

As the scattered flakes of snow thickened into a steady stream, they decorated the tree in between sips of mulled wine, bites of fruit cake, and much laughter. By the time they'd finished, the harsh contours of the city lay buried under a billowing cloud of softness. Turning off all the lights but those on the tree, they stood close together at the window, gazing at the luminescent glow of the street lamps.

Mikhail's breath was warm against the top of her head as he murmured, "If anyone had told me I would actually come to like snow . . . But then, I could never have imagined being here with you, feeling as I do. . . ." Tilting her head back, he stared at her for a long moment before gently touching his mouth to hers.

With their arms around each other, they settled down on the couch in front of the fire to sip more wine and talk. Exactly when the conversation petered out into contented silence Erin didn't know.

Nor could she say when her head nestled against his broad chest or her eyes fluttered closed. Sometime during the night she was carried to bed, her outer clothing gently removed, and a warm quilt tucked around her. A soft smile curved her mouth as Mikhail dropped a tender kiss on her forehead. As though in a dream she heard the quiet murmur of his voice saying, "Sleep, sweet angel."

As she slipped away into a dream she missed his low masculine chuckle as he added, "While you can!"

# Chapter Six

$\mathcal{T}$he warm, relaxed mood continued between them the next morning as they shared an early breakfast. Over the poached eggs Mikhail had prepared and Erin's best bran muffins, she felt comfortable enough to admit, "I was worried about you when I got home and found you weren't here. All sorts of crazy thoughts went through my mind."

Mikhail nodded apologetically. "I should have left a note, but, to be truthful, I'm so unaccustomed to someone being concerned about me that I didn't think of it."

"Oh, I understand that. When you walked in I felt foolish for having let my imagination get the better of me. But for a while there . . ."

"What worried you, Erin? Was there anything specific?"

"Yes, in a way. . . . Perhaps it will sound ridiculous to you, but I actually found myself wondering if your country's regime might not regret releasing you and might try to prevent you from speaking out now that you're free."

"That is not at all ridiculous," Mikhail said quietly, "but I had hoped it would not occur to you. It's unlikely they would even make an attempt; if I thought otherwise I would not be staying in your apartment. But the possibility does remain that something might be tried out on the street, where an assailant could quickly disappear into the crowds."

His calm acceptance that his life could be in jeopardy dismayed Erin. The mere thought of him being forced to suffer more pain than he already had, or perhaps even being killed, sickened her. "How can you speak of it so matter-of-factly? Don't you want to do something . . . get some sort of protection?"

He reached across the table to take her hand gently in his own, his touch comforting. "There is no protection, Erin. This above all I have learned over the last year. If a tyrannical, amoral power is determined to destroy you, there is nothing you can do to stop it. However, it *is* possible to make the cost of that destruction so high that the very pragmatic men who make such decisions will decide against it."

"How?"

"By speaking out. I realize that my arrival in this

country has been kept very quiet in order to give me time to get my bearings and settle in a bit. I appreciate that, but I don't think I should delay any longer before making a public statement. Not only do I owe it to all the people still in prison in my homeland, but it is also the surest way of guaranteeing my own safety. Once I have put myself in the public eye, so to speak, it will be far too risky for them to try to silence me."

"I see . . ." Erin murmured. What he said made sense: If his government did try to eliminate him after he had spoken out, they would only be lending added credibility to his charges. Once she understood how a press conference could enhance his safety, she was anxious for one to be arranged as quickly as possible. But when she suggested that the State Department would be the appropriate place to go for assistance in dealing with the media, Mikhail disagreed.

"I must not appear to be too closely associated with any government, otherwise the authorities in my country will simply use that as an excuse to discredit everything I say. No, this must be done independently, with only representatives of the media and myself involved. That is why I am hoping you will agree to help me." He hesitated before adding, "But perhaps it would present a conflict of interest with your position on *Focus*."

"Not at all," Erin assured him quickly. "Since *Focus* is a weekly news magazine, rather than a daily, we concentrate on more in-depth coverage of the issues. That's what led to my series of articles about you; they really weren't the sort of thing a newspaper or TV station could have done. We're not in competition with them at all, so I don't see how anyone could object to my helping you arrange a meeting with their representatives."

Privately, she wasn't as confident as she sounded. When Derek heard about Mikhail's plans he was going to be more than a little upset. It would take careful handling to make him see that any help they could give the expatriate writer would only improve the magazine's stature, but Erin told herself she could pull it off. After all, she had to. Mikhail's reasons for holding the press conference were far too important for her to let anything get in the way.

Unfortunately Derek didn't agree. "Why would you want to help him with that?" he demanded as they confronted each other across the wide expanse of his desk later in the day.

Erin smothered a sigh. She had just spent half an hour trying to explain how much they could benefit from assisting Mikhail, but so far she had made little progress toward convincing the managing editor. Derek was proving distressingly obstinate. He refused to see beyond the fact that she wanted to reveal a story that he regarded as exclusively the magazine's own to other reporters.

Although he understood perfectly well how Mikhail would increase his safety by putting himself in the public eye, he claimed not to consider that to be top priority, at least not when compared to the all-important goal of staying out in front of the competition.

Nor did the fact that Mikhail felt compelled to speak out in support of the people still being held in political prisons particularly move him. It was too bad about those poor guys, and he'd certainly like to be able to help them, but the smart man didn't let sentiment get in the way of his own best interests.

Erin got the distinct impression that he wanted to be convinced, but only in some way that didn't undermine his tough-guy image. In desperation she resorted to her final argument. Remembering that Derek had long coveted the Editor of the Year award bestowed by his colleagues in the media, and that he had been nominated yet again that year, she said, "Of course, if you did agree to the press conference it would certainly take the air out of Ed MacElroy's sails."

At the mention of his nearest rival for the award Derek straightened slightly. "You think so?"

"Definitely. In fact, you might even say it would be a really dirty trick to pull on him. After all, doesn't MacElroy try to present himself as the dean of editors, the statesman of the business and all that? What's more statesmanlike than helping a writer of Mikhail Demertov's stature speak out on an issue of international importance?"

Derek thought for a moment, his broad forehead furrowed in concentration. "It might just work. . . ." Catching the triumphant gleam in her eye, he quickly added, "I know perfectly well that you're trying to manipulate me, Hennessey. Ordinarily I wouldn't let you get away with it, but this time you do have a point."

"Does that mean we can hold the conference here?"

With the decisiveness that had marked his abrupt rise in the industry, he nodded. "You damn well better, since I plan to be the one who introduces Demertov and sets the stage for whatever he has to say. Let's see . . ." Leaning back in his chair, he pictured the scene. "The boardroom upstairs should be perfect. It's classy but low-key and will hold a good-size crowd. Check with building maintenance to make sure the wiring can support the TV lights and cameras. How long do you think he plans to talk before we open it up to questions and answers?"

"I don't know."

"Will he come across well on camera?"

"I have no idea."

"Can he field the questions a mob of reporters are likely to throw at him?"

"Beats me."

Derek scowled. Ignoring the delectable vision she presented in a red wool suit with her umber hair hanging loose around her shoulders and her high-boned cheeks slightly flushed, he sent her his most intimidating look. His frown deepened as she returned his gaze imperturbably. "Has it occurred to you," he demanded, "that you are not particularly well prepared to cope with a major publicity event?"

"That's not how I think of it. We're talking about

people's lives and freedoms, not the introduction of a new brand of corn flakes."

"Call it whatever you want, the fact remains that when Demertov gets up there our prestige is going to be on the line."

Erin translated that to mean that Derek's chances for the award, and quite possibly her job, would be at stake. She didn't care a fig for the first, but the second was important enough to make her refrain from giving vent to the anger his loused-up priorities provoked.

As calmly as she could she said, "Then I'll go ahead and make the arrangements. I've already suggested to Mikhail that tomorrow afternoon would be the best time to hold the conference. That will assure coverage in the morning and afternoon papers on Christmas Day, when the story should have maximum impact."

"Not bad," Derek drawled. "Ever think of a career in journalism?"

"Is that what this is? I thought we were just generating a little publicity to improve our image."

"Put a lid on that fine Irish temper, Hennessey, and keep your mind on business. That'll work out best for everyone involved, including the illustrious Mr. Demertov."

Though she hated to admit it, she knew he was right. Derek was far too astute to do more than subtly exploit the news conference. He knew full well that at the first sign of blatant self-promotion his colleagues in the media would turn on him with a vengence and take great pleasure in shredding both his reputation and his career.

That being the case, she could count on him demonstrating precisely the right degree of sincere concern. What Mikhail would make of his presence, she couldn't guess, but she was certain that, after having come through so much, he wouldn't let one ambitious editor get in the way of what he planned to say.

After returning to her office she asked Jenny to put through a call to building maintenance while she began assembling a list of those who would be invited to attend. Derek's secretary, Sheila, had offered to do the telephoning, for which Erin was grateful. She wanted to concentrate on coming up with a series of probable questions to help Mikhail prepare his responses.

Though most of the newspeople were likely to treat him with more than the usual degree of respect and courtesy, there were bound to be some who would consider it a matter of honor to play devil's advocate. She was determined to do everything possible to minimize their verbal attacks and assure that the key points Mikhail wanted to get across would be fairly reported.

By noon she had made enough progress to return home. As she came in the door she was surprised to hear voices in the living room. Mikhail was seated on the bed wearing gray wool slacks that emphasized the long, hard line of his hips and thighs. A periwinkle blue sweater hugged the firm breadth of his chest. Beneath it a gray-and-blue plaid shirt was open at the collar, revealing the beginnings of the thick mat of golden curls that covered his torso. His hair was freshly trimmed; just enough had been taken off to bring out the rugged strength of his features more clearly. He looked so uncompromisingly male that Erin was helpless to prevent the sudden surge of excitement that darted through her. She barely noticed the earnest young man seated in a chair across from him who jumped up when she entered.

Mikhail rose also, but with none of the other's anxiousness. He beamed her a warm smile. "Ah, Erin, I have been wondering when you would get back. Let me introduce Mr. Chester Robeson, of the State Department."

Taking a steadying breath, she managed to nod politely. "I hope I'm not interrupting . . . ?"

"Of course not," Mikhail assured her. "I was just explaining to Mr. Robeson that I am in excellent hands and that, much as I appreciate his interest, I really do not need any further assistance."

Erin frowned slightly. The State Department had already agreed to let Mikhail stay with her. There was no reason that she knew of for anyone from the government to be checking up on him.

"Is there some particular matter you came to discuss?" she asked the young man quietly.

Robeson's prominent Adam's apple bobbed up and down as he nodded. "Well, yes, in a manner of speaking, there is. But first let me say how delighted we are that Mr. Demertov is settling in so well. Frankly, some of us at the Department were a bit concerned about the idea of a civilian, so to speak, looking after him. But you seem to be doing a splendid job, Miss Hennessey. Just splendid."

Ordinarily the young man's pompousness would have amused her, but Erin was beginning to feel more than a bit uneasy. She was no stranger to public officials who tried to mask unpalatable suggestions in a mass of flowery compliments.

"I'm sure you're a very busy man, Mr. Robeson, and you *have* come all the way from Washington, so don't feel you have to stand on ceremony. Why don't you just explain why you're here?"

The words were said politely enough, but there was an undercurrent of firmness in her tone that made it clear that the explanation had better be good. Robeson frowned uneasily. "Actually, Miss Hennessey, this matter is between Mr. Demertov and myself. I don't quite see how you're involved. . . ."

"She is involved because I say she is," Mikhail explained quietly. Taking Erin's arm, he led her over to the couch and sat down next to her. Robeson had no choice but to accede to her presence. Nonetheless he stubbornly directed his comments to Mikhail.

"As I was explaining when Miss Hennessey arrived, we at the Department are very anxious to assist you in any way we can. While we understand that you prefer to remain in New York, we would like to arrange some time with you to discuss conditions in your homeland, most particularly in the labor camps."

"You want to debrief me?"

"Well, yes, I suppose you could put it that way. It is the accepted procedure with defectors of your stature."

Mikhail smiled wryly. "I am not precisely a defector, Mr. Robeson. To be absolutely correct, I was expelled. Not, I hasten to add, that I am not very happy to be here, no matter how I arrived. Naturally I will provide all the information I have that may be of assistance to the people still in my country's political prisons. However, please do not expect me to tell you anything that could be used against the general population."

The State Department man's eyes narrowed. Leaning forward slightly, he said, "I don't get the distinction, Mr. Demertov. You're out, so what difference does it make what you tell us?"

"A great deal, to me. I will not be a party to causing difficulties for the ordinary people of my country; they already have all they can cope with in trying to survive under a repressive regime."

"But those people are a big chunk of the problem, Mr. Demertov. After all, by failing to stand up against your government, they make its abuses possible."

Robeson smiled slightly, as though confident that he had raised an incontrovertible point. But Mikhail merely shook his head. "You are trying to oversimplify a very complex issue. Wasn't there a popular slogan in this country awhile back to the effect that if you are not part of the solution, you are part of the problem? Laudatory sentiments, until you realize that if you carry them to their logical conclusion you can end up justifying anything that is done to people who happen to be caught in the wrong place at the wrong time. That is the reasoning of terrorists, Mr. Robeson, not sane men."

Reluctantly the young man backed down, but only slightly. "I can see that you're in something of a quandary. Naturally you don't want to be responsible for possible injuries to an innocent person. But believe me, Mr. Demertov, there's no reason for you to be concerned. Our government will never misuse any information you give us."

Erin muttered something rude under her breath, but Mikhail merely looked amused. "Your faith is rather touching, but I do not share it. Governments come and go, and even when they are of the best possible caliber, there can always be a few—what do you call them?—bad apples that spoil the bin. I have had rather dramatic experience with how easy it is for information to be transformed into a weapon that, in the wrong hands, can wreak enormous damage. Regretfully, Mr. Robeson, I stand by my original statement. Any information I can give you about the labor camps, you are welcome to. But nothing more."

The politely sincere look that had marked the young man's expression throughout the exchange faded. A petulant scowl marred his forehead beneath thinning hair of an indeterminate color. "Where I come from, Mr. Demertov, that's called plain ingratitude."

Erin opened her mouth to deliver the dressing down she was convinced he richly deserved, but

Mikhail forestalled her. Quietly he asked, "And where precisely do you come from, Mr. Robeson? That very impressive identification card you waved in front of me could have been printed up in any number of places."

That was enough for Erin. She stood up quickly and headed for the phone. "I'm calling a contact of mine at the State Department. If they didn't send this guy, we'll find out right away."

"Hold it," Robeson muttered. He had slumped on the couch, staring at them with mingled frustration and annoyance. "There's no reason to make a big thing out of this. I just told you I was from the State Department because that seemed the easiest way to get you to talk to me."

Mikhail raised one eyebrow skeptically. "Wouldn't it be more accurate to say you knew that if you told the truth I wouldn't be inclined to let you into the apartment, much less talk to you?"

Sighing, Robeson nodded. "Look, it's not easy working for the C.I.A. We have a real image problem."

"C.I.A.?" Erin repeated. After just about deciding that he was either an agent for Mikhail's government or a rival reporter, she had to do a rapid reordering of her thinking.

Mikhail had no such problem. He appeared completely unsurprised by the young man's disclosure. "I've been expecting you. Why did you wait this long to show up?"

Robeson shrugged. "We were trying to be discreet."

"You didn't succeed very well." Smiling cordially, he stood up. "I will explain this only once more. My gratitude to this country is immense. I will do everything I can to express my appreciation up to the limits of my own conscience. Beyond that I will not go. I trust that I am making myself clear, Mr. Robeson?"

The young man nodded glumly. He picked up his briefcase and turned toward the door. "I'll put that in my report, Mr. Demertov. But don't expect my superiors to be happy about it. They figure we have a lien on you, and they mean to collect."

After he had left Erin shook her head disbelievingly. "I thought there wasn't much left that could surprise me, but that was incredible."

"Unfortunately it is also all too common. Mr. Robeson is a considerable cut above his colleagues in my country, but he operates from a similar willingness to exploit anyone for any reason. The irony of it is that I really don't possess any information that could possibly be of use to his organization, but he would never believe that."

"I hate to sound naive, but there is a law against the C.I.A. operating inside the United States. What just happened here was strictly illegal."

"I'm glad to hear it. That means Mr. Robeson and his ilk will be very sensitive to the possibility of public exposure, so it becomes even more urgent for me to hold that press conference as quickly as possible. Were you able to make any progress on that?"

Erin nodded. Quickly she explained the arrangements. When she was through, she added, "Since you can expect to draw some of the top reporters in the country, it might be a good idea to hold a dress rehearsal, so to speak."

"Rehearsal? I don't understand. What is there to rehearse?"

"Whatever you hope to get across to the media and, through them, to the public. No one who can avoid it confronts reporters without first giving a lot of time and attention to predicting what they'll ask and preparing the best possible responses."

Mikhail still looked skeptical. "How can you anticipate the questions other reporters will ask? After all, aren't the members of a free press likely to pose any inquiry that occurs to them?"

"Certainly, but since I have some experience with such situations myself, it isn't especially hard to guess what questions will arise. Not all of them, of course, but a good number."

"The leaders of your country commonly do this? They prepare their answers in advance?"

"Absolutely. Everyone does it, and not because they're trying to hide anything, although that does sometimes come into it. More often it's because we all recognize that in the heat of the moment, when the television cameras are whirring, dozens of microphones are turned on and reporters are shouting questions from every side, it's very easy to forget an important point or put something in such a way that it might be misunderstood."

"Yes . . . I can see how that would be the case. . . ." Mikhail thought it over for another moment before nodding. "All right, if you think it's a good idea to have this 'rehearsal' then we will do so."

They were quickly settled in front of the Christmas tree, making short work of coffee and sandwiches as she described the arrangements for the conference.

Erin was careful not to mention the difficulties she had encountered with Derek, because she didn't want to add in any way to the tension she was certain Mikhail must already be feeling. But some measure of her impatience with the managing editor must have gotten through, because he said, "It sounds as though your boss presented some problems. Was that the case?"

"Yes," she admitted reluctantly, "a few, but you shouldn't be concerned about that. Derek feels the conference is very important, and he'll do everything he can to help." She saw no reason to add that his cooperation stemmed in large measure from self-interest.

As they began to go through the questions and answers, she was relieved to note that for someone who had never before addressed the media, he showed a remarkable grasp of how to tailor words and ideas to get the most attention focused where he wanted it.

Long before they were finished, Erin had no doubt that the conference would make headlines. The full weight of public condemnation would be brought to bear on the suffering he had experienced and that countless others continued to suffer.

She also learned far more than she had ever

wanted to know about the human capacity for brutality. Even as she marveled at the extraordinary courage and spirit that had enabled him to triumph over seemingly insurmountable obstacles, she knew that the images his words unleashed would haunt her forever.

After they retired again to their separate bedrooms Erin lay awake far into the night. Not until shortly before dawn did she manage to slip into an uneasy sleep that did little to prepare her for the day ahead.

# Chapter Seven

Fifteen minutes before the news conference was due to begin, Derek met them in the small waiting area behind the boardroom. Erin had to give him credit; he looked the epitome of the intelligent, committed executive.

The gray pin-striped suit and light-blue shirt he wore were perfectly suited to television and projected just the right image of conservative elegance. His thick chestnut hair was brushed back with a seeming casualness that was appropriate for a man far too busy to fuss over his appearance. The judicious use of the tanning room at his health club had given his skin a burnished glow.

As he strode into the room he exuded an air of

utterly unshakable command that wavered only slightly when he came face to face with Mikhail.

The understated luxury of the dark blue suit that had arrived that morning from Brooks Brothers should have made them no more than equals in appearance. But while the editor's sartorial elegance caught the eye, Mikhail's did not. All such superficial details were blocked out by the sheer impact of the man himself.

His courage, sensitivity and determination were obvious to even the least observant eye. As the two men surveyed each other Derek's eyes narrowed speculatively. He glanced from the tall, powerful man who was looking him over quietly to Erin, standing close beside Mikhail's side. A slight frown furrowed his brow. With a smile that made no pretense at warmth, he offered his hand. "Mr. Demertov . . . welcome to the United States. It's a pleasure to meet you."

Without giving Mikhail a chance to respond, he turned to Erin. "Can he understand what I'm saying? His English is good enough for that, isn't it?"

Unperturbed, Mikhail said quietly, "My English is more than adequate, Mr. Kent. You need not be concerned about that." Though he spoke with perfect courtesy, he somehow managed to make it sound as though Derek were unduly nervous and worrying over trifles.

Erin fought to hide a smile that she knew would only worsen an already tense situation. For reasons she didn't care to explore, her boss seemed bent on the hopeless task of trying to establish his superiority over a man he could never hope to best.

"Just checking," Derek muttered. "Once those old boys in there get going, you're not going to know what's coming at you. Try to stay cool, and don't say anything you don't want to hear spewing out of a TV tonight or read about in tomorrow's papers."

"I'll keep that in mind," Mikhail said dryly.

The level of noise reaching them from the board-room might have dismayed a lesser man, but he showed no flicker of concern. Certain of both the importance of the information he intended to present and his ability to communicate it clearly, he said, "I understand you have offered to introduce me to the media, Mr. Kent. May I suggest we do that now, since from the sound of it they are, as you say, chomping at the bit?"

Derek's scowl deepened, though whether from annoyance with the other's man's insurmountable confidence and ability, or simply because he didn't like having control of the situation taken from him, was impossible to say. Nodding curtly, he led the way into the boardroom.

As they entered, the cacophony momentarily lessened, only to surge back more powerfully than ever as the reporters bandied first impressions of Mikhail back and forth among themselves, while some of the more aggressive hurled questions which he politely ignored.

Derek took his place at the dais, straightening his tie. He gave the cameramen a few moments to adjust their lights and lenses, and photographers for various newspapers and magazines began snapping off what were likely to be the first of many rolls of film.

When the noise had subsided to a polite hush, he began. "Ladies and gentlemen, my colleagues in the news media, I am honored to welcome you here today, and I am gratified by your attention to a matter of truly worldwide importance. As many of you know, efforts have been under way for several months to secure the release of Mikhail Demertov, a highly respected dissident writer, from prison in the Communist bloc and to bring him safely to the United States. A few days ago his government abruptly agreed to free him in an apparent attempt to improve its bargaining position regarding certain trade agreements now in negotiation. Mr. Demertov was transferred to Paris and then flew immediately to New York; he arrived here earlier this week. Now that he has had a chance to rest up a bit, he is prepared to make a statement about his incarceration and to answer your questions. Mr. Demertov . . ."

After stepping away from the dais, Derek went to stand beside Erin. Relieved that none of his personal resentment of the other man had come through in his introduction, she was feeling more kindly disposed to him. Together they watched as Mikhail stepped forward to the dais. Cameras clicked away furiously and reporters pressed closer, anxious for a good look at a fellow writer who exemplified the finest ideals of their profession.

Removing a single page of notes from his pocket,

he glanced out over the audience as he said, "First, I wish to express my thanks to both the United States government and the many private citizens of this country and others who were instrumental in securing my release. Without their assistance I have no doubt that I would still be imprisoned, my writings banned, and my voice silenced. But grateful as I am to be here with you today, I cannot lose sight of the fact that I am only one man, and that thousands of others continue to suffer brutal oppression and abuses against humanity that must not to be tolerated by any free people."

Quietly but firmly he went on to outline the conditions in the prisons of his homeland and to charge that prisoners were subjected to both physical and psychological tortures designed to destroy all resistance. Long periods of solitary confinement were common; Mikhail himself had lived completely alone in a tiny cell for six months.

Forced labor projects were the norm. After his captors had decided that his spirit could not be broken by isolation, he had been moved into the general prison population, where he toiled eighteen hours a day in the frigid Arctic winter, building a pipeline that was intended to deliver natural gas to customers in the western part of the country.

He had seen men die of exhaustion, starvation and exposure. Others had been crushed by the brutally dehumanizing conditions and became human automatons, no longer capable of thought or reason. But resistance had continued. The love of freedom was too great to be destroyed even by such ruthless oppression. Despite all the horrors he had described, he concluded on a note of optimism, with the hope that the struggle for human dignity would continue even against the most overwhelming odds.

The silence when he finished was an eloquent testimony to the impact of his words. Very little could impress a horde of reporters strongly enough to win even a few seconds of quiet, let alone the long, drawn-out hush that followed his statement.

The faces turned toward him were grim, each man and woman confronting the possibility that but for an accident of birth they might have been the ones to suffer such persecution. Implicit within each was the uncertainty whether or not they would have been among those who survived, or whether they would have joined the countless, nameless mass of victims who perished because of their ideals.

In that atmosphere of silent self-examination and empathy for those less fortunate than they, the questions began.

A reporter from one of the television networks raised the issue that was undoubtedly uppermost in everyone's mind.

"Mr. Demertov, why, in light of your outspoken opposition to your government and your determination to expose its violations of human rights, were you chosen to be released? Wouldn't it have been wiser, from the point of view of your country's leaders, to have selected someone less likely to take such a public position?"

"Yes, it certainly would have been," Mikhail agreed quietly. "But there were compelling reasons for my selection. Many of my fellow prisoners were in such poor mental and physical condition that it would not have been necessary for them to say anything in public. They bore mute evidence of their suffering, which nothing could have hidden. I, on the other hand, was fortunate enough to come through my imprisonment in relatively good condition. Also, because of the efforts of people in the West, I had become a very visible symbol of oppression. By freeing me it was hoped that some of the outrage directed at my government would be defused. Of course, I intend to do everything possible to make sure that does not happen."

"You've made very serious charges against your government," a newspaper reporter pointed out, "but you haven't offered any evidence other than your own word that these things are happening. Is there documentation to support what you say?"

"Yes, I am certain that such proof exists. The forced labor projects that I know about are all of importance to the security of my homeland, so they would be logical targets for examination by your spy satellites. Such surveillance would be bound to reveal that the people working on the projects are prisoners, and that the conditions they are compelled to endure are brutalizing in the extreme. Moreover, photographs and reports about the conditions of prisoners have been smuggled out to the West. There is no lack of evidence."

"Why, in your opinion, is your government so determined to continue the oppression?" a correspondent for one of the major wire services asked.

"Wouldn't it be prudent to allow at least a small degree of freedom, rather than take the risk that, by keeping the lid on so tight, they may force things to a point where they will eventually blow up in their faces?"

"Not when you consider that my country is really a confederation of many diverse states populated by different ethnic groups, many of whom have no love for each other. My government presumes that people are essentially untrustworthy and should be allowed as little power as possible. Yours operates from the belief that people will more often than not have the strength and courage to look beyond self-interest and do what is best for the larger good. Sometimes that works and sometimes it doesn't. But at least here you get to try. In my homeland everyone is a prisoner of our fundamental lack of faith in each other, which has caused us to place all power in the hands of despots."

As he paused for a moment to wipe away the perspiration caused by the intense heat of the television lights, Erin studied him closely. His composure was undented. Neither the strain of the rapid-fire interrogation of the reporters nor the painful memories he must be reliving showed on his chiseled features. He continued to look out at the audience calmly and determinedly. No one who saw and heard him could doubt that he was a man who believed absolutely in what he was doing.

But at least one person who watched him was determined to shake his confidence, for reasons that became clear as soon as the young man identified himself as a representative of *The People's Press.* "Isn't it true," he demanded stridently, "that far from being the freedom fighter you would like us to believe, you were in fact arrested for being an agent of the C.I.A. and that you are still in the pay of that organization?"

Instead of reacting angrily, as he might have been expected to, Mikhail simply laughed. "I would have thought that by now the people responsible for my imprisonment would have been able to come up with a better excuse for it. Speaking as one writer to another, you should know that charges of C.I.A. involvement are the worst sort of cliché. You would be well advised to freshen up your act if you expect to have any chance of undermining my credibility."

As the rest of the media representatives chuckled the young man flushed. Even more loudly he insisted, "Then how do you account for your obvious affluence? You're clearly getting money from somewhere."

Mikhail frowned slightly, and Erin knew that he was wondering exactly how many aspects of his personal affairs were known to the representatives of his government and the people they chose to speak for them. Quietly he said, "There is a marvelous invention here in the free world called author royalties. For years my books have been smuggled out of my homeland to be published in the United States and elsewhere. Their sales have been gratifyingly large, and my publisher has been commendably conscientious about depositing my earnings in various bank accounts." He added humorously, "I know it's expected for writers to complain about being poorly paid, but in my case, I genuinely have no quarrel with either the reading public or my publisher. In fact, I owe them both my thanks."

Having neatly turned what might otherwise have been a serious threat to his credibility into a joke, Mikhail went on to answer several dozen other questions from reporters who had no axes to grind.

As he did so Derek leaned closer to Erin and muttered, "I should have figured that's where the money was coming from. Let's not have any more surprises like that. From now on I expect you to pin him down on every question and every lead. By next week I want one hell of a wrap-up story on my desk. Got it?"

Reluctantly Erin nodded. She sensed that she had pushed Derek as far as she could, and that he wouldn't give another inch, especially now that he had met Mikhail and seen for himself the other man's indomitable strength and determination. Unless she wanted to see the story turned over to another reporter, she had better produce it quickly.

Ordinarily that wouldn't have posed any problem, but with Mikhail, she knew that she would have to struggle to maintain the objectivity that was so vital to good journalism. Silently she wondered how she could manage it when each moment with him led her deeper into an emotional and sensual maelstrom from which she had not the slightest wish to escape.

# Chapter Eight

*Y*ou did a bang-up job, Demertov," Derek announced grandly when the conference was over and they were all settled in his office with a round of drinks. "I can't remember the last time I saw a mob of reporters take to anyone like that. You can count on some very complimentary coverage."

"I appreciate that," Mikhail said quietly, "but I am not looking for compliments. If they simply relay the facts I will be more than satisfied."

"Sure, sure. But it doesn't hurt to know who's on your side and who isn't. That little creep from *The People's Press,* for instance. I'd like to find out how he got in there."

"It was an open conference," Erin reminded him.

"We knew perfectly well that word of it was bound to spread beyond the people we actually invited, and if we had tried to bar journalists we thought would be unfriendly, we would have caused a storm of protest."

"I suppose," Derek muttered. "But he still came close to doing some damage with that C.I.A. charge. It's not quite the cliché we'd like to think."

Mikhail glanced at the other man skeptically. "Are you saying that people in the United States would take such an accusation seriously?"

"No, probably not. Or, if they did believe it, they'd be likely to think you hadn't done anything wrong. But you're trying to convince other people besides Americans of what you say is going on in your country. Europeans, for instance, would tend to take charges of C.I.A. involvement very seriously indeed."

"Perhaps. . . . But at any rate, there is nothing I can do about it. If my government is determined to air such a ridiculous accusation, it will do so, no matter what I say."

"You should at least be prepared to go on denying it," Derek insisted.

"I do not agree. If I continue to protest my innocence I will only draw more attention to the charge itself. No, from now on I intend to concentrate on my writing and whatever else I can do to help those still in political prisons."

The managing editor frowned, not at all pleased to have his advice so summarily dismissed. He was accustomed to having his recommendations gratefully received, not rejected out of hand.

Perhaps because of that, or simply because he didn't like the warm looks that had been passing between Erin and Mikhail since the conclusion of the news conference, he said, "I hope that doesn't mean you don't want to give any more interviews, because Erin is counting on a big story from you."

Mikhail's silvery eyes widened slightly before becoming just a bit guarded. "Oh? I was not aware that *Focus* planned any further coverage of me." .

Shaking his head ruefully, Derek laughed. "Well, now, I can't imagine how she forgot to mention that to you. Did it just slip your mind, Erin, honey?"

The angry disbelief that had seized her the moment she realized he intended to mention the story to Mikhail broke through to the surface. "No, Derek, *sweetheart,*" she snapped. "It didn't slip my mind, as you know perfectly well, since we just talked about it again not ten minutes ago. Or did you forget that I promised to deliver the article next week? That is . . . if Mikhail agrees to give me the information I need."

Glancing over at him worriedly, she was half afraid of the displeasure she might see in his eyes. Considering his past experiences with betrayal and exploitation, he might be excused for wondering how much of her interest in him was genuinely motivated by personal feelings and how much stemmed from her determination to stay at the top of her profession.

A moment later Erin breathed a sigh of relief as he said, "I will be happy to provide any assistance I can with the story. In fact, since it is due next week, perhaps we should get started right away."

Telling herself that she should have realized Mikhail was far too perceptive and intelligent to fall for such an obvious attempt to cause trouble between them, she agreed at once. They left Derek's office a few minutes later.

Outside, Erin introduced Mikhail to the staff members who had gathered in the hope of meeting him. She had to bite back a laugh as Jenny gazed up at him adoringly, and even the usually cool Sheila did an excellent impression of starstruck awe. But the smile faded as she realized that their admiration was as much for the man himself as for the immense talent he possessed.

Having already felt the full force of Mikhail's potent attraction herself, she could hardly deny that he affected other women just as powerfully. From the most hard-boiled reporter to the most impressionable copy girl, no one was immune to his appeal. A tight knot of apprehension grew in her stomach as she wondered what the odds were that a man so long deprived of female companionship was likely to want to settle down contentedly with one woman when he could so easily sample many.

That thought remained with her as they finally left the building and started walking up Fifth Avenue. It was snowing again, and the street was crowded with last-minute shoppers. The City seemed to have called a brief truce with its residents. Even the traffic police were smiling as they worked to keep the endless flow of cars moving, if not quickly, at least smoothly. The pungent aroma of chestnuts roasting over open fires and the joyous pealing of church bells high up in the steeples of St. Patrick's filled the air.

Mikhail had taken her hand in his and shortened his long stride to match hers. They walked along in what would have been a contented silence if Erin hadn't been feeling the full force of her insecurities and doubts about herself as a woman.

It didn't take long for him to realize that something was wrong, although he wasn't sure what. Gently he asked, "Erin, that meeting with your editor . . . it didn't distress you, did it?"

"What? Oh, no, of course not. I was annoyed that he felt called upon to mention the story I want to do, but that's standard procedure for Derek. He always shoots from the hip."

"Shoots from the hip?" Mikhail repeated, savoring what was for him a new expression. "That's very good. I can figure out what it means without ever having heard it before. And yes, you are quite correct. He strikes me as the sort of man who would behave that way."

"Always," Erin said dryly. "He's an expert at bullying people verbally, or, at least, most people. I noticed he didn't seem to faze you."

"Did you think he would when he mentioned the story?"

"Yes . . . it did cross my mind."

Shaking his head, Mikhail smiled down at her. "We are both writers, so I have no difficulty understanding how important your work is to you. And even if I did not, I still would not presume that you should give up all professional interest in me just because we have become personally involved."

The slightly husky timbre of his voice and the warm look in his eyes made Erin's throat tighten. Hesitantly she said, "Are we . . . personally involved?"

"Oh, yes," Mikhail declared without the slightest doubt. "And we are going to be even more so." His gaze darkened as he added, "I think you already know that, regardless of your relationship with Kent, I intend to have you for myself."

This startling announcement, uttered with blatantly male confidence, stunned Erin. She was struck by both his misinterpretation of her involvement with the managing editor and his frankness about the role he meant to play in her life and opted to deal with the easier part first. "But I only work for Derek. There's nothing personal between us."

Mikhail frowned. "He called you honey, and you called him sweetheart."

"And you thought that meant we were involved outside the office?"

"What else was I to think?"

Laughter bubbled up in Erin. "That was just sarcasm. Derek knows it bothers me to be called by pet names in such an inappropriate setting, so he does it whenever he's really annoyed. And I finally got so tired of it that I decided to do the same to him."

"I thought that might be it," Mikhail admitted, making no effort to hide his relief, "but with English not being my native language, I couldn't be sure. Not that it makes any difference," he added matter-of-factly. "You are a woman well worth fighting for."

Never having thought of herself in such a decidedly primitive way, Erin couldn't quite suppress a little shiver of feminine pleasure, but she felt compelled to struggle against it. "That doesn't sound very liberated. You wouldn't be a closet male chauvinist, would you?"

"Not at all. But neither am I so foolish as to believe that because men and women are equal, we are also identical. There are still very powerful forces at work in us that no amount of social change can alter."

As though to demonstrate the truth of what he had just said, Mikhail stopped suddenly and drew her into his arms. Before she could even begin to object his mouth claimed hers in a soul-searing kiss that drove out all thought of protest. Oblivious to the crowd of shoppers who smiled at them indulgently, he took her on a long, thorough exploration of the senses that didn't stop until they were both breathless.

When at last he lifted his head she was flushed and wide-eyed. The rapid rise and fall of her breasts was visible even under the heavy wool coat she wore.

Brushing a snowflake from her upturned nose, he laughed softly. "Beautiful Erin, you are as lovely as the island you were named for. Certainly your eyes are as green, and sometimes as sad. You must know I will not do anything to hurt you."

She nodded mutely. Not for a moment did she think Mikhail would ever intentionally harm her. But she also realized that when such overwhelming emotions were released, it wasn't always possible to predict what would happen. Even as she accepted the fact that she was set on a course she couldn't bear to abandon, she had to wonder where it would lead her.

As they covered the remaining few blocks home, the snow grew steadily heavier. By the time they reached the apartment house where Erin lived they could see only a couple of yards ahead. Traffic was thinning out rapidly as the last shoppers hurried home. There was a hushed, expectant quality to the crystalline air that Mikhail had no difficulty in sensing.

Pausing outside the ornate art-deco lobby, they knocked the snow from their boots as he asked, "Is it always like this at Christmas? As though you are all waiting for something important to happen?"

"I guess it is," Erin said slowly, entering the elevator. He had put into words something she had only been able to sense. "Even though we're commemorating an event that took place almost two thousand years ago, it retains such a sense of mystery and wonder that it's impossible to remember clearly from year to year. It has to be captured each time as though it had never been experienced before."

"There are other experiences like that," he murmured, unlocking the apartment door.

She turned, gazing up into the quicksilver glimmer of his eyes. "Like what?"

A burnished finger touched her cheek gently. "Every time I feel the softness of your skin, hear your voice, smell the perfume you always wear, I think I will remember the sensation. But I cannot, at least not completely. Each time, I rediscover you all over again." He laughed softly as she dropped her gaze self-consciously. "You are a remarkable collection of complexities. Today, at your office, I saw the calm, collected journalist and businesswoman, and she impressed me very much. But there is another part of you I have also seen, the soft, yielding part that has come to haunt my dreams."

Unwilling to meet his eyes even when he tilted her head back, Erin laughed shakily. "It's no wonder your books have such impact, Mikhail. You have the soul of a poet."

"Thank you," he murmured, "but I have no need of poetry to express what I feel for you. I have only to say the truth." Quietly he added, "And you have only to accept it."

Still Erin could not respond. Her thoughts were in too great a turmoil. The yearnings he set off in her body threatened to overwhelm her, but they were as nothing compared to the ache in her heart. Never would she have thought it possible for any man to so effortlessly undermine her defenses and make her want to completely disregard the teachings of a lifetime.

With Mikhail she forgot to be prudent, forgot to worry about the future, forgot even that she had never intended to know a man intimately without first being certain that they shared a mutual commitment to each other. All that mattered now was that they come closer and closer until at last even the barriers of physical separation would dissolve so they could be truly one.

Shaken by the force of her own emotions, Erin instinctively backed away from him. Correctly gauging the dismay in her eyes, Mikhail let her go, but only as far as the kitchen. While she started dinner he turned on the tree lights, pulled the curtains and got a fragrant log going in the fireplace. When she returned with a simple but delicious meal of steaks, salad, freshly baked French bread and a hearty red wine, the room had taken on a soft glow that relaxed her almost against her will.

They spoke little as they ate. Erin was caught up in her own thoughts, struggling to decipher feelings and actions that were so out of character for her that they might have belonged to a stranger. She had no doubt about where the intimate dinner in front of the fireplace was leading. Some new level of decisiveness that she sensed in Mikhail warned her that he had no intention of waiting much longer.

Nor did she try to fool herself into believing that she wanted to delay what she yearned for so irresistibly. Silently she acknowledged that she had reached the point where all the forethought, analysis and reason in the world had to be jettisoned in favor of the powerful inner voice that was telling her to yield to her most fundamental needs. The time had come to trust her instincts and her heart.

They cleared the dishes away together and returned to settle down once again in front of the fire. Mikhail took off his jacket before adding a fresh log to the blaze. Erin watched as the finely woven linen of his shirt stretched over the sculpted muscles of his arms and back. His movements were startlingly graceful for so large and powerful a man. His hands, lifting the heavy log as easily as though it were a matchstick, were big and lightly sprinkled with golden hair. The memory of their calloused but gentle touch shivered through her.

A pulse began to beat in the slender column of her throat. Her gaze was drawn irresistibly downward along the taut length of his tapered hips and sinewy legs. Without her being aware of it, her sea-green eyes grew soft and slumberous, giving her an alluringly seductive look.

As he turned back to her the firelight darkened his hair to burnished copper while emphasizing the hard lines and shadowy planes of his face. She couldn't make out his expression, but she did hear his sharply indrawn breath as he surveyed her sensual beauty.

While working in the kitchen she had discarded the jacket of her turquoise wool suit, leaving her in only the softly draped skirt and a delicate cream silk blouse trimmed at the collar with handmade lace. Her hair, which had begun the day in a neat chignon, had come undone to tumble around her shoulders. Her high-boned cheeks were faintly flushed from the heat of the fire, and from her thoughts.

He stopped, staring down at her from his great height. She thought she must have imagined the slight trembling of his hands when at last he moved toward her again. "Erin . . ." he breathed softly as he sat down beside her on the floor, close to the fire. "I can't quite convince myself that you aren't a dream."

Startled, she gazed back at him. "A dream? No, I'm not a dream. . . . You are. . . ." She laughed shyly, unable to stop herself. "I used to dream about a man like you . . . strong, tender, intelligent. . . . I had almost given up hope that you really existed. But you do . . . and you're here. . . ."

A tender smile curved his hard mouth as he raised a hand to gently cup the back of her head. His fingers tangled in the silken strands of her hair, drawing her closer. "Then, if we're both dreams, let us share the night, sweet Erin; I can't bear to be without you any longer."

A feather-light kiss touched her brow before his lips moved slowly down along the curve of her cheek to the lobe of her ear. She gasped as he nipped her gently, only to instantly soothe the tiny hurt with his tongue. Waves of pleasure undulated through her, washing over and drowning the last faint remnants of reason.

Moaning softly, she moved deeper into his embrace, giving herself up to his impassioned touch. Yet even as he took her mouth completely, his big hands stroking circles of pleasure along her silk-covered back, she was certain of the absolute control he maintained over himself. Though she no longer had any doubt that this time there would be no drawing back for either of them, she trusted Mikhail to go slowly and make the experience as perfect for her as she wanted to make it for him.

As he trailed a line of fire down her throat to the scented hollow at the base of her collarbone, he lowered her gently to the carpet. Stretched out beneath him, her body engulfed by the overwhelming size and strength of his, Erin knew for the first time in her life the sensation of being truly vulnerable. Yet the knowledge that he could easily overpower her brought no fear. Implicit in it was the realization that his strength would soon be joined to hers as together they found a union far beyond anything they could ever experience as individuals.

A heady sense of her own femininity coursed through her, prompting her to return his caresses in kind. As his mouth claimed hers again she met him in an erotic duel that presaged what was to come on an even more intimate level.

Mikhail groaned deep in his throat. Holding her firmly with one hand, he slid the other up to cup the fullness of her breast. Through the thin silk of her blouse, his mouth nuzzled the pouting nipple, his tongue rasping over it in a motion that ignited bursts of flame deep within her.

She cried out softly, kneading the taut muscles of his back. Knowing only that she couldn't bear to be separated from him by even the thin layers of their clothes, she pulled his shirt from the waistband of his slacks and slid her hands under it, savoring the unyielding warmth of skin over steely muscles.

The quiver of pleasure that coursed through him warned her that his need was every bit as great as her own. No thought of resistance remained in her when he pressed her back into the soft rug and determinedly unfastened the buttons of her blouse. It fell open to reveal her low-cut bra, little more than a scrap of lace that hid nothing from his eyes. They glowed like molten silver as he unclipped the front fastener, feasting on the beauty laid bare before him.

Erin shivered helplessly from the heady combination of passion and fear. She wanted so desperately to please him, but she was struck by doubt about her ability to do so. Seeing the uncertainty in her eyes, he murmured huskily, "Undress me, Erin. I need to feel your hands on me."

Tremulously she obeyed, pushing aside the smooth linen of his shirt to reveal the massive expanse of his chest. A soft gasp broke from her as she yielded to the compelling need to learn his body as thoroughly as he was learning hers.

Tentatively at first, then with growing confidence, she stroked the flat male nipples that hardened at her touch. Breathing in the heady scent of his sandalwood aftershave combined with the potently male essence of his body, she smiled enticingly. Her lips caressed the velvety expanse of muscles covered by thick golden curls as her tongue darted out to taste him.

Mikhail shook with the impact of her touch. A deep rumble like the breaking of waves on a distant shore rose from his chest. All the carefully erected barriers that had sheltered his heart and spirit through the long, treacherous years were cracking wide open. Rays of golden light pierced him, making him almost cry out in exaltation.

Moving swiftly, yet with infinite gentleness, he unfastened her skirt and stripped it from her, along with the silken pantyhose and blouse. Her bra followed, leaving her in only a tiny fragment of lace guarding the juncture of her satiny thighs.

Modesty mingling with desire made her flush. Bending over her, savoring her exquisite loveliness, Mikhail laughed softly. "You are exquisite . . . so perfect in every way. Every inch of you is so beautiful. . . ."

Driven close to mindlessness by hungers she had never even imagined, much less experienced, Erin moaned softly. "Please . . . I need you so badly. . . ."

Mikhail heard her plea and echoed it. Taking both her hands in one of his, he guided them to the buckle of his belt. "Then free me for you, Erin. Let there be nothing between us but our own flesh."

Her fingers fumbled with the supple leather, but she managed to undo it and to unfasten the button of his waistband. Beyond that she could not go. She had to endure his indulgent chuckle as he pulled down the zipper and swiftly tossed away all but his briefs.

Staring at him as he loomed over her in the

firelight, Erin breathed in sharply. He was so un-compromisingly male that he unleashed her most primeval feminine urges. When he came down beside her, stroking the silken smoothness of her body, she moaned softly. His hands moved slowly from the swelling fullness of her breasts down the incline of her waist to the flat expanse of her abdomen, where they tightened on her hips. Huskily, he murmured gentle words of desire and reassurance.

His deep, tender voice soothed her even as his touch excited her unbearably. Trembling, she reached out to stroke the hair-roughened length of his thigh as it eased between her slender legs. His skin was hot beneath her fingers, and she could feel the acute tension tightening his muscles.

When his fingers reached beneath the delicate rim of her panties she jerked slightly, but lay quietly as he removed them. The almost reverent admiration glowing in his silvery eyes touched her deeply. Without hesitation she opened her arms to him.

Mikhail gathered her into his embrace, cradling her against his massive length. Well aware of how easily he could hurt her if he went too quickly or roughly, he caressed her with slow, gentle strokes that made her quiver helplessly.

Slipping his hands beneath her, he squeezed her buttocks as he let her feel the full extent of his arousal. A soft gasp broke from her, followed instantly by a rippling purr of contentment as his mouth captured the taut peak of her breast to suckle her with gentle fierceness.

Launched headlong into an ecstatic flight toward

some shimmering peak she could barely envision, Erin yielded utterly. She was barely aware when he lifted her high against his chest, capturing her lips with his as he carried her into his room. When he laid her on the bed she shivered in the sudden coolness that vanished the instant his body returned to hers.

No trace of the embarrassment she had felt earlier remained to dim her pleasure as she realized that the last barrier separating them was gone. Luxuriating in the ardent proof of his desire, she moved instinctively to bring them even closer.

As her legs fell open he slid between them with all the naturalness of a homecoming. His tongue plunged deeply within the moist cavern of her mouth, his hands gently kneading and stroking the aching fullness of her breasts.

Waves of sensation piled one upon the other until she thought she couldn't possibly bear anything more. But Mikhail had other ideas. Determined to savor every inch of her, he slid down her body, raining heated kisses along the delicate line of her ribs, into her dimpled navel, across the silken smoothness of her belly to the ultrasensitive skin of her inner thighs.

Overwhelmed by spiraling coils of pleasure that threatened to explode at any moment, Erin abandoned herself to his most daring caresses. Writhing beneath him, she became a wild thing, swept by repeating flashes of ecstasy that melded together into a firestorm of need.

When Mikhail moved away from her for a moment she cried out in protest. He soothed her with a gentle caress even as he held his own desire at bay long enough to protect her.

The realization that he could think of her well-being at such a time shattered her last thin hold on restraint. She welcomed him back joyously, an ecstatic cry breaking from her as he at last made them one.

Holding himself still within her, Mikhail waited until he was certain that she had adjusted to his intimate possession. Only then did he move slowly and gently to bring their pleasure to a shattering crescendo.

Swept by irresistible convulsions, Erin cried out his name. His features were tightly drawn, and his eyes glowed with the light of inner flames as their gazes locked. Mikhail was fully with her in that timeless instant, an instant torn out of all the rest of existence and made purely their own. Together they ascended to the furthest limits of ecstasy before shattering in an incandescent burst of release.

Consciousness slowly re-formed as they drifted back down to earth. Erin lay still, barely breathing, luxuriating in the sensation of his weight still holding her to the bed. When he thought to move, worried that he might be crushing her, she stopped him with a gentle touch. "Stay . . . please. . . . You feel so good."

His mouth curved in a smile against her silken skin. "I can't possibly feel any better to you than you do to me, my beautiful Erin." Raising his head enough to look into her eyes, he murmured, "I never knew it was possible to experience such joy."

Knowing that she was only telling him what he already knew, she couldn't resist the urge to whisper, "Neither did I. Nothing could have prepared me for this."

Mikhail laughed deep in his throat, an utterly male sound of satisfaction. "And I am very glad nothing did. You are mine now, Erin. Only mine."

His fierce possessiveness sent tiny echoes of remembered pleasure shimmering through her. Lovingly entwined in his arms, she slipped away into a sleep deeper and more content than any she had ever known.

# Chapter Nine

Something was tickling Erin's nose. Refusing to open her eyes, she eased a hand out from under the covers and batted at it desultorily. Instead of going away, as any self-respecting feather or whatever it was should have done, it grew more persistent. A soft sigh escaped her as she was finally forced to admit that she was awake.

Her eyelids fluttered once, twice, then snapped wide open as she realized that Mikhail was gazing down at her, teasing the tip of her nose with a strand of her hair.

"Good morning," he murmured, smiling as he took in her confusion, which gave way almost instantly to memories that made her blush.

"Oh . . . uh . . . good morning. . . ." Sitting up

slightly, she clutched the covers to her breasts as she gazed at him in mingled disbelief and astonishment. Had the previous night really happened? Had she really lain in his arms and been transformed into the impassioned creature she remembered?

The intimacy of their bodies lying close together under the sheet and a lingering sense of languid well-being told her that it had been no dream. Nor could she summon the faintest hint of regret. Gazing into Mikhail's silvery eyes, drinking in the sight of his stubble-roughened cheeks, tousled hair and powerful chest visible above the covers filled her with delight.

Long moments passed before she realized that he was watching her closely, apparently searching for belated pangs of conscience or remorse. Instinctively she reached out to reassure him. "I'm so glad you're here," she murmured softly, "and so glad we're together."

His relief was complete and unfeigned. He smiled broadly and kissed her lightly on the nose before climbing calmly out of bed. "That calls for breakfast, or at least coffee. Are you hungry?"

Distracted by the sight of him standing naked in the dim light filtering through the curtains, she could only nod. Not for the world could she tear her eyes from him as he shrugged into a terry-cloth robe, then held out a large flannel shirt for her.

Realizing that he meant for her to leave the protection of the sheet she still clutched, Erin hesitated, but only for a moment. The tenderly mocking grin he shot her forced her to swallow the remnants of the modesty that had somehow managed to survive the unbridled passion of the night before. Stepping quickly toward him, she reached for the shirt, only to have him hold it just beyond her grasp as his powerful arm wrapped around her and drew her close.

Breathing in the fresh scent of her hair, he said softly, "You must not be shy around me. Your body is exquisitely beautiful. It gives me great pleasure to see you like this."

His words and the arousing touch of his body combined to send a thrill of pleasure through her. Standing on tiptoe, she gently touched her lips to his. The caress conveyed appreciation for his reassurance, and far more. As they stepped slightly apart, Mikhail holding the shirt open for her, their eyes met in shared agreement that they would soon be back in the big, welcoming bed.

But first there was the ritual of Christmas morning to enjoy. As he made coffee and slipped half a dozen croissants into the oven, Erin quickly retrieved the presents she had stashed in her closet and slipped them under the tree. After turning on the lights she took a peek out the window. The blizzard that had struck the western states with such fury had descended on New York.

The city was having a truly white Christmas. Through the swirling clouds of snow she could barely make out the buildings across the street. Cars left parked along the curbs were already beginning to disappear. The branches of the trees were etched in white, and front stoops had vanished under fluffy, wind-tossed blankets. Nothing moved for as far as she could see. Nature had decreed a rare moment of tranquility where there was usually none. Erin meant to enjoy it to the fullest.

She turned back just as Mikhail came into the room. His eyes widened as he spied the presents that had appeared under the tree. "What is this?"

She shrugged teasingly. "Beats me. It looks as though Santa Claus dropped by."

"E-rin . . ." He tried to sound stern, but failed completely. The delighted, almost little-boy, look that lit his face was reward enough just by itself.

From across the width of the room he gazed at her tenderly, his expression so open and vulnerable that her throat tightened. "Just a moment," he said. "I'll be right back."

Puzzled, she wondered what he was up to. Her question was quickly answered when he returned with his arms laden with gaily wrapped packages.

Laughing, Erin shook her head ruefully. "Mi-khail . . ."

"I had nothing to do with this," he claimed as he placed the presents under the tree. "A very large man in a red suit left them."

Sitting side by side on the couch sipping their coffee, they made an effort at decorum. But they kept glancing at the pile of gifts and at each other, until, like giddy children, they could wait no longer.

"You first," Erin insisted, holding out a package wrapped in silver paper and tied with a large red bow.

132

He began to open it eagerly, but slowed down when he realized what he was holding. Carefully he turned the large leather-bound book in his hands. "I have always wanted to read Thoreau, but his works are banned in my country. Now I will finally have the chance. Thank you, Erin."

It didn't seem possible that anything could make her feel happier at that moment, but she quickly discovered that her assumption was mistaken. The package Mikhail selected from under the tree and handed to her contained a delicate, intricately carved gold locket that she knew at first glance was an antique. It appealed to both her sense of beauty and her love of the past. Everything about it said that it had been chosen with special care, and that touched her as much as the gift itself.

"Thank you," she said softly. "I'll always treasure this."

His touch was gentle on the back of her neck as he lifted her hair away so he could secure the locket. When it was in place he sat back slightly, studying her. Erin met his eyes calmly. A deep sense of contentment and purpose was growing in her. She hugged it to her, instinctively understanding that she might well need it later when the full enormity of what was happening to her sank in.

But for the moment, at least, there was only more laughter and enjoyment as the rest of the presents were unwrapped. Her guess that Mikhail would want books had proved correct. He was delighted with the works by John Steinbeck, Ernest Hemingway and Thomas Paine that she had selected. Added to the books she had already noticed accumulating around his desk, they made the beginning of a good collection.

Just as she had chosen gifts that she knew would fulfill his yearning for knowledge he had been denied, his presents paid tribute to the utterly feminine part of her nature that was usually constrained by her high-pressured, professional world.

In addition to the locket there were a crystal flask of her favorite perfume, a jade comb for her hair and, last but hardly least, a white silk and lace peignoir that was at once intensely romantic and unmistakably sensual.

As she lifted it from the box Erin couldn't resist the impulse to ask, "When did you choose this?"

Mikhail's grin told her that he knew exactly what she was thinking. "Several days ago. You see, I was determined that you would be mine, and once I make up my mind about something, I am not easily deterred."

"I can hardly claim to have led you much of a chase," she murmured, her eyes still on the gossamer fabric she held. It was so light that she could barely feel it. Against her body it would be little more than a tantalizing cloud, hiding almost nothing from his gaze.

"Does that distress you?" Perceptively he had guessed that the swiftness of her surrender might be an embarrassment to her.

Erin nodded reluctantly. She wasn't about to try

to explain to him that what was happening between them challenged her most deeply held beliefs and values. She would never have thought it possible for her to become so intimately involved with any man on such short acquaintance. Whenever she had tried to imagine how the love she hoped for would come into her life, she had envisioned a slow progression from friendship to far greater commitment. Instead she had encountered an explosion of passion and desire for which she had been completely unprepared. It made her feel acutely vulnerable, but still she couldn't stop herself from responding with all the warmth in her generous nature.

"It shouldn't," he said quietly. "There are a few irresistible forces in this world that can never be controlled. We seem to have encountered one of them. To try to slow it down, to channel it in any particular direction, would be not only futile, but possibly destructive."

Erin heard the warning implicit in his words and understood it. He was a man who nurtured many ideals, but no illusions. He recognized the immense difficulty of trying to knit together two lives as disparate as their own, but he was also very clearly determined that they would overcome the challenges their relationship presented.

She took comfort from his resolve even as her own determination rose to match it. Smiling, she said, "All your gifts are beautiful, Mikhail, but last night was the most beautiful of all. Nothing will ever equal it."

Too late she realized that the words could be taken as a challenge. The utterly male gleam in his eyes told her he had chosen to interpret them as just that. Reaching for her, he murmured, "You think not? Then I shall have to convince you otherwise."

Flustered, she tried to draw back. "I was going to take a shower. . . ."

Her tentative objection left him unperturbed. Rising, he lifted her effortlessly into his arms, then strode down the hallway toward the bathroom. "That's an excellent idea."

There was something deliciously exciting about being carried off like that, Erin decided. Her stomach fluttered softly in anticipation even as the wantonness of her imaginings brought a rosy glow to her skin. Seeing her blush, Mikhail laughed. "I hope you never try to bluff your way out of any situation. Your every thought shows on your face."

"I always did have expressive features," she murmured, far more interested in the hard sweep of his chest beneath her cheek and the warmth of his gaze as he scrutinized her tenderly than in her own words.

After he had set her on her feet in the blue-and-white tile bathroom, Erin stood motionless as Mikhail turned on the shower. Her eyes never left his when he reached for the buttons of her shirt, undoing them and gently easing the covering from her. His own followed swiftly. She had barely a moment to admire the long, lean sweep of his body before he took her hand, and together they stepped under the stream of pleasantly hot water.

A world of new sensation opened for Erin. She had thought that she had experienced the ultimate in her body's capacity to feel, but she had been wrong. As the heated mist rose around them Mikhail led her on a rapturous voyage beyond anything she could ever have imagined.

His palms gently cupped her swelling breasts as he dropped feather-light kisses along the curve of her cheek, over the bridge of her upturned nose, down across the slender line of her throat. When at last he met her mouth with his, she moaned softly. Their tongues touched, stroking in a provocative rhythmn that made her tremble.

The thick mat of golden hair covering his chest felt like silk beneath her fingers as she yielded to the need to touch him. Slowly, savoring every moment, she followed the sculpted hardness of his chest up to his massive shoulders, stroking the hollow at the base of his corded neck before reaching up to trace the rugged planes and angles of his face.

Her finger teased his mouth gently, only to be teased in turn as he suddenly drew it into the moist cavern, nipping gently.

"Mikhail . . ." The rush of water almost drowned out her voice, but it couldn't dim the ardent look in her emerald eyes. It was answered by his own as he drew her closer, the urgency of his need making her arch against him.

Bending his head, he slowly, tantalizingly, flicked his tongue across her taut nipples, teasing first one and then the other until she thought she would surely go mad from the sensation. When he finally drew one into his mouth to suckle her gently she trembled uncontrollably.

The sense of her own womanly power that he had awakened in her the night before demanded that she give pleasure as well as receive it. Tentatively at first, then with growing assurance, she let her hands and mouth wander over him until he groaned in delight.

"I was wrong, Erin," he muttered huskily as he gently put some slight distance between them. "You are not an angel, but a sorceress. Much more of your magic and I will be undone."

Elated by her ability to stir him so intensely, she laughed confidently. "Would that be so terrible?"

"No, but I prefer that it be in bed." A devilish gleam entered his eyes as he added, "Later, when we are more accustomed to each other, I will be happy to explore other alternatives with you. But just now . . ."

She didn't hear the rest of what he said. Her imagination had taken over, conjuring up visions that turned her face bright red. Mikhail laughed heartily at her reaction. "You are a delightful bundle of contradictions." Picking up the soap, he began to work up a lather between his hands. "How many women are both genuinely shy and gratifyingly eager?"

Erin could hardly deny that she was either. It was too much of an effort to even speak. She could only stand docilely before him as he gently but thoroughly bathed her. No spot on her body was missed by his careful, insistent touch. On the sensitive skin of her breasts and inner thighs he used his hands. Everywhere else he rubbed her vigorously with the rough-textured loofah until her body glowed.

When he was finished he handed the soap and cloth to her, and she hesitated for only a moment. The need to touch him overwhelmed all else. Tentatively at first, then with growing assurance, she explored his body as thoroughly as he had hers.

Framed by immense shoulders and arms, his back was a long sweep of powerful muscle and sinew leading down to the flat, hard planes of his buttocks. His skin might once have been pale, but long exposure to the elements had darkened it to a warm bronze that contrasted vividly with his golden hair.

Taking a deep breath, she murmured for him to turn. When he did so their eyes met for an instant. His were slumberous with a passion so intense as to send a shiver of anticipation through her, but she was still not yet ready to give up her enthralling explorations. This was her first opportunity to really see his body, and she intended to make the most of it.

The sculpted muscles of his chest fascinated her, as did the lean hardness of his flat belly and the tensile strength of his thighs. Golden hair covered his torso and tapered down past his narrow waist.

So enthralled was she by the enticing differences between them that she only gradually became aware of the scars that added a poignant note of vulnerability to his male beauty. Her face paled as she took in the mute reminders of experiences that she couldn't bear to contemplate. Trembling, she blinked hard in a futile effort to hold back the sudden rush of tears that turned her eyes to sea-washed pools.

"Erin . . ." Mikhail's voice was a husky whisper, barely audible above the cascade of water. "Do not cry. . . ." He touched a gentle finger to her cheek, catching the diamond droplet.

"I can't help it. . . . It hurts to think of you being hurt."

Gathering her closer, he soothed her with a gentle caress. "That part of my life is over. From now on there is only freedom and a chance for happiness beyond anything I could have imagined. Think of that, Erin, not of what is done with."

She knew that he was right, but it was still difficult to forget all he had endured. Driven by an instinctive need to comfort him, she nuzzled her head into the breadth of his shoulder. The silken weight of her hair drifted through his hands and over the rippling muscles of his arms. Her breasts brushed against him gently, the taut peaks hardening further as they encountered the thick mat of hair covering his chest.

All thought, all reason, all doubt, slipped away from her, and she let them go without regret. The need that had driven her into his arms the night before was now even more intense. Later there might come a time to look back and regret, but just then she could do nothing but savor the wonder of what was happening between them.

Mikhail seemed to share her awe. Gently, as

though he feared she might vanish from right between his hands, he lifted her out of the shower. After being wrapped in a big, fluffly towel she was carefully dried from the top of her glistening hair to the bottoms of her feet.

When he was done she returned the favor just as scrupulously. She could feel the tremors of desire racing through him even as he forced himself to remain quiet under her touch. The hard lines of his face were drawn almost painfully taut when at last she dropped the towel and stood before him, proud in her nudity and confident of the pleasure she could give.

Mikhail's silvery eyes swept over her, piercing her with the sheer male intensity of his approval. His look left no doubt that everything he saw delighted him. The low growl of demand he gave as he pulled her to him rumbled to the very core of Erin's being.

As he swept her up into his arms again she laughed softly. "I could get very used to being carried off like this."

He grinned down at her rakishly. "That's good, because I intend to keep right on doing it."

The implication that he considered their relationship to have a future wasn't the absolute declaration of intent she would have liked, but it still reassured her. There was no hint of restraint or doubt in her response when he laid her on the bed and came down beside her swiftly.

As their limbs lovingly entwined Erin surrendered to the overpowering sensations he unleashed within her. Their union of the night before had taught her much about her own body and his. Now she added to that knowledge. Not content to merely receive pleasure, she was determined to give it as well. His surprise when she pressed her hands against his shoulders, urging him onto his back, gave way instantly to wholehearted approval. Guided by instincts as old as humanity, and emboldened by Mikhail's obvious delight, she gently but persistently nourished his passion until at last he could bear nothing more.

Turning swiftly, he positioned her under him. His mouth and hands teased her to a level of pleasure so intense that it teetered on the edge of pain. Her head tossed wildly back and forth on the pillow, her hair streaming out in a silken fall around them. Every cell of her body was acutely sensitized, every nerve ending primed and ready. When he entered her at last she cried out in relief that gave way instantly to even more intense waves of desire.

Slowly, persistently, he drove her toward a shimmering explosion of fulfillment. The ecstatic denouement was almost upon her when he suddenly pulled back. Erin cried out in longing, reaching for him, only to have Mikhail elude her grasp.

"Be patient," he groaned into her mouth, the husky quality of his voice revealing his own acute arousal. "I want this to be perfect for you."

Gasping, she tried to tell him that it already was, but the words wouldn't come. She was beyond speech, beyond thought, capable only of responding to the electrifying sensations that were spreading through her in undulating waves that carried her higher and higher with each passing moment.

His return to her body was swift and even more forceful than before. Arching her hips, Erin moved with him, perfectly matching his rhythmn. They soared together, coming ever closer to the final burst of ecstasy on which her consciousness now focused. But despite the completeness of their joining, she was still powerless to stop him when he withdrew yet again.

"Oh, no . . . please. . . ."

Mikhail could answer her only with his eyes. His quicksilver gaze was on fire with unbridled passion and determination. His breath came in harsh gasps and his skin glistened with perspiration. The powerful muscles of his chest and arms were tightly clenched. Yet the hands that touched her were infinitely gentle, and the lips that claimed hers offered the promise that the enthralling torment would soon end.

Emboldened by passion so intense as to make even the thought of restraint unendurable, she stroked the broad sweep of his shoulders and chest, reaching down along the taut muscles of his hips and thighs. Mikhail groaned, and a hoarse gasp broke from him when at last she touched him intimately.

"Bring me to you, sweet Erin. Show me that your need is as great as mine."

No fragment of resistance hindered her as she moved to do his bidding. The utter rightness of their lovemaking banished all inhibition, and a joyful sigh escaped her as they came together in shattering completeness. Their flight reached beyond the boundaries of time and place to join them totally in exhilarating union. Their very souls seemed to meld in the instant when the world exploded around them and reality became only their two bodies locked together and their two hearts beating as one.

# Chapter Ten

"Play in the snow?" Mikhail repeated dubiously. "Are you sure that's what you want to do?"

Erin smiled at him from across the breakfast table. They were enjoying a rather late brunch of blueberry pancakes with maple syrup, thick rashers of bacon and freshly squeezed orange juice. After a long, languorous morning spent in bed she was ravenously hungry.

"Absolutely. Not only is it a lot of fun, but I think it's time I got to introduce *you* to a new experience instead of the other way around."

Mikhail laughed gently. She watched him, thinking how she loved the way his eyes lightened when he was amused and how tender his mouth looked when he smiled. Sighing inwardly, she admitted to herself that there was no getting around the fact that she was deep in the throes of infatuation.

Everything about him beguiled her. Every word and gesture was a source of endless fascination. Moment to moment his impact on her grew. She could hardly believe that he was real, much less that he was sitting just across the table from her wearing only a terry-cloth robe that hid little of the lean, hard body that had so thoroughly enthralled hers throughout all the magical hours of the night and early morning.

The simple act of lifting a forkful of pancakes to her mouth was almost too much for her despite her hunger. The only consolation lay in the fact that Mikhail seemed equally bemused. In the midst of refilling their coffee cups he became distracted by the play of light across the curve of her cheek and let the hot liquid slosh onto the table. As they both scrambled for towels to mop up the spill their eyes met teasingly.

"We'd better go out," Mikhail said, "before we wreck this place."

"Why do you say that? Just because I burned the first batch of pancakes, we almost threw out the orange juice instead of the peels and the floor still smells of the maple syrup we spilled?"

"That and the fact that I could swear I saw steam rising from the bed." Laughing at her blush, he kissed her lightly. "Let's give it a few hours to cool off while you convince me there's something good about snow."

Half an hour later, warmly dressed in boots, ski

pants and down-filled jackets, they left the apartment. The blizzard had stopped during the night after dumping more than a foot of snow on the city. Plows had cleared the major avenues, but the side streets were still heavy going. Erin was glad of Mikhail's help; he easily lifted her over drifts that came almost to her waist.

People were beginning to emerge from the buildings wearing the outwardly blasé but inwardly pleased air of adults temporarily catapulted back into childhood. With all the offices and stores that had planned to be open the day after Christmas suddenly shut down by the weather, there was no possibility of working or running errands. The only thing left to do was to go out and play.

Already enterprising street vendors were doing a brisk business in sleds. "We have to get a red one," Erin insisted as she and Mikhail stopped to look over the selection.

The wiry young man who was selling them sighed. "They're all the same, but no one wants to buy anything but red. Even these real nice silver jobs aren't moving too well." He looked at them hopefully, but Erin shook her head.

"It has to be red," she repeated. "All the sleds I've ever had were red. I'm not sure anything else would work."

Shrugging at the vagaries of fate, which made apparently intelligent people believe that gravity wouldn't function the same way when confronted by a blue or yellow or silver sled, the young man pulled a large red one out of his pile.

"It's kind of heavy," he warned, only to break off as Erin's very large companion tucked it effortlessly under one arm.

As they strolled toward Central Park Mikhail's slate-gray eyes lightened in the way Erin already knew meant that he was thinking of something pleasant. Seeing her quizzical look, he explained, "I had a sled just like this when I was about eight years old. My parents and I were living in Paris. We used to go to the Bois de Boulogne for sleigh rides." He smiled wryly. "I haven't thought of that in years. It was a very happy time."

Glad that she'd had some part in helping him to remember the enjoyable experiences that had been temporarily hidden beneath all the pain and treachery marring his adult years, Erin squeezed his hand gently. A sense of companionship too deep for words enveloped them as they walked farther into the park.

The oasis of natural beauty in the midst of Manhattan's glass and steel towers lay buried under a pristine blanket of white, transformed into a fantasy realm of magical shapes and otherworldly vistas. White-jacketed tree branches stood out clearly against the periwinkle sky. Sunshine reflecting off the crystalline banks filled the air with liquid light. A clean, crisp wind blew out of the north, reddening their cheeks.

Because he wore no hat, Mikhail's golden hair ruffled slightly in the breeze. His features were more relaxed than Erin had yet seen them. The last few days seemed to have stripped years from him, restor-

# Waldenbooks

43 SALE 0534 0464/1 05/26/85

| | | | | |
|---|---|---|---|---|
| 0440129605 | 3 | 1@ | 2.95 | 2.95 |
| 0373107986 | 3 | 1@ | 1.95 | 1.95 |
| 0373027001 | 3 | 1@ | 1.95 | 1.95 |
| 8 PREMIUM | 100% | | | 1.95 - |

```
SUBTOTAL                        4.90
MICHIGAN 4% TAX                   .20
TOTAL                           5.10
PAYMENT                         5.10
CHANGE                           .00
```

SO MUCH MORE THAN A BOOKSTORE

05/26/85  16:36

ing a measure of the youthful exuberance and optimism that were a fitting accompaniment to his vast intelligence and courage. His resiliency amazed her, even as she understood that it was his ultimate gesture of defiance against the system that had tried to destroy him.

She had difficulty remembering that barely a week before he had been facing a life sentence in a brutalizing prison camp. Seeing him now, it was possible for her to believe that he had never confronted any problem greater than what normally occurred in the course of a talented, ambitious life. Only when she gazed into his eyes did she see the shadows that nothing would ever erase completely.

Following a path of beaten-down snow, they reached a large, gently sloping hill already dotted by brightly colored sleds. Mikhail shook his head ruefully as they watched the exuberant crowd of children and grown-ups. Laughing down at Erin, he said, "I have a feeling I'm about to experience a side of you I haven't encountered yet."

"You mean something other than the incredibly astute reporter and the seductive *femme fatale?*" she teased.

His eyes were softly indulgent as he nodded. "I can see the little girl you used to be. She's a charming sight."

Laughing self-consciously, Erin tugged at his hand. "Come on. Let's climb to the top."

They had to wait their turn before at last being able to position the sled at the edge of the slope.

Erin nestled in front of Mikhail, whose arms wrapped around her while his long legs were stretched out on either side of hers. At her signal they both threw their combined weight forward. Their downward progress began slowly enough, but quickly picked up speed. Within seconds they were hurtling headlong toward the bottom of the hill, the air tearing at them and the ground careening up at full tilt. Landing in a snowbank, they tipped off the sled and rolled a few feet, ending up in a tangled heap.

Cushioned against Mikhail's big body, her eyes glowing and her whole being suffused by a radiant sense of well-being, Erin laughed delightedly. "That was great! Let's do it again."

He groaned and made a show of humoring her, even though it was clear that he was enjoying himself every bit as much as she was. Hand in hand they tromped back up the hill, only to come flying down it again moments later. That ride was followed by another and another, until they were both covered with snow, their faces red and their smiles as broad as any child's.

When they were at last briefly satiated, they left the sledders and joined a group building a snowman. Or at least Mikhail helped with it. Erin, the other women and a cluster of little girls insisted on making a snowwoman. Theirs turned out much better, to the chagrin of the men and boys, who promptly challenged them to a snowball fight.

Mikhail joined in with some reluctance, apparently concerned that the women might be hurt. He quickly discovered that their aims were every bit as good as the men's. When Erin hurled a snowball that hit him squarely in the chest he didn't hesitate to retaliate. His deft throw knocked the wool hat from her head. As she turned to retrieve it he tackled her from behind, sending them both rolling into a snow-drift.

"No fair!" she protested, unable to restrain her giggles. "Let me up!"

"Not until you pay a forfeit," he insisted with a menacing gleam in his eyes.

"What for? I hit you fair and square."

"No you didn't. I would have ducked, but you're so beautiful that you distracted me. I claim a penalty."

Though she had a very clear idea of how much she would enjoy the punishment he intended to mete out, Erin continued to make a show of outrage. "Oh, no! I'm not giving an inch."

His powerful head bent toward her as he growled, "Then I will just have to take what I want."

For all his pretended fierceness, the lips that teased and coaxed her own were infinitely gentle. Lying beneath him in the snow, her breath coming fast and hard, Erin was helpless to deny her response. Like a flower opening to the sun, she strained toward him, meeting the proprietary thrust of his tongue with a fervor that matched his own.

The velvet roughness with which he stroked the tender inner flesh of her mouth sent waves of fire spiraling through her. She moaned softly deep in her throat, and his powerful arms slid beneath her to cradle her protectively even as he drew her further and further into an inexorable web of pleasure. The barriers of their clothing and the relative lack of privacy restrained them somewhat, but even so, all her senses were on fire with need by the time he reluctantly drew away.

"I think," Mikhail muttered thickly, "that we should go home."

Erin nodded, too dazed to speak. He helped her up and they dusted each other off beneath the indulgent glances of the opposing teams, who didn't have to be told that the snowball fight had just lost two participants. The sun was beginning to slant below the winter-bare branches etched against the western sky as they left the park, once again hand in hand.

They were barely inside the apartment with the door locked behind them when their clothes began to come off. Their boots and jackets were left in a pile in the entry hall, while the distance to the bedroom was littered with sweaters and shirts.

Her hands worked quickly at the buckle of his belt as Mikhail unzipped her slacks and pulled them from her. They tumbled across the bed, savoring the taste and touch of each other. After unfastening her bra he tossed it onto the floor, then gently cupped her breasts in his big hands. His tongue flicked repeatedly over the nipples as Erin arched beneath him, moaning softly.

The arousal that had begun to build while they'd been in the park was increasing so swiftly that she couldn't bear sustained lovemaking. On fire with need for him, she stroked the hard length of his back as her slender legs entwined with his.

Sensing her urgency, which he fully shared, Mikhail quickly stripped the last garments from them. He waited only long enough to be sure that she could receive him before bringing them together in a shattering explosion of ecstasy that hurtled them both beyond the furthest limits of consciousness.

Only much later, when she had recovered sufficiently to speak, did Erin murmur, "If that's what playing in the snow does for us, I'm going to pray for a long winter."

Rolling over, Mikhail grinned down at her. "I'll join you. I had no idea a blizzard could result in such fun."

They lay together in a warm, contented heap until hunger of a different sort finally drove them to dress in dry clothes and make their way to the kitchen. Once dinner was started they settled down to read about Mikhail's press conference, which was prominently featured on the front pages of the major papers. The staid morning paper declared "Expatriate Writer Charges Human Rights Violations" while the more brazen evening tabloid trumpeted "Exiled Author Blasts Commies."

The coverage was even more detailed than Erin had hoped. Sidebar stories accompanying the report on the conference described the history of oppression in the Eastern bloc and quoted the responses of other exiles living in the West. The consensus seemed to be that Mikhail had accurately described a brutal system of persecution that had existed for decades and was growing steadily worse.

"Is it my imagination," Mikhail asked as they set the table, "or were the reports of what I said somewhat slanted in my favor?"

"There were a few paragraphs that went a bit beyond the usual standards of objective journalism," Erin admitted. "But that isn't surprising. Any writer listening to what you described is bound to feel intensely sympathetic. It's a real 'There but for the grace of God go I' situation."

"Is that how you feel?"

She hesitated, unsure of how completely she wanted to reveal the complex and almost frightening emotions he aroused in her. "I'm trying to follow your advice and not dwell on what you've been through," she said at last. "It's just too painful for me at this point. But before, when you were still in prison and no one could be certain that you'd be freed, I did sometimes wonder how well I would do in a similar situation. The only answer I came up with is that it's impossible to tell without actually experiencing it."

"I understand what you are saying," Mikhail told her gently, "but I think you are underrating yourself. You possess a rare sense of strength and courage that I believe would serve you well under any circumstances."

Deeply moved by his quiet words, Erin nonetheless felt compelled to ask, "How can you be really sure of anything about me when we've known each other such a short time?"

"Are you suggesting I should doubt you?" he shot back, the hint of a smile curving his mouth. "No, Erin, I will not accept that. Our acquaintance, brief though it has been, is too intense to allow for any of the usual pretenses people hide behind. Whether you are ready to admit it yet or not, we have come to each other honestly."

Biting her lip, she considered what he had just said. Was he fully aware of how quickly he had become a vital part of her life and of how vulnerable that made her feel? And if he was, could she also take his words to mean that the emotions she thought she saw in him, all the tenderness and understanding he had shown her, were completely genuine and unfeigned? Was it possible that he had really learned to care for her so greatly in such a short time?

Unwilling to voice the questions out loud, Erin had to be content with silent rumination. Caught up in an extraordinarily emotional and sensual experience, she understood that any attempt to make sense out of what was happening to her was bound to fail, but even so, the more reasoned part of her mind insisted that she try.

Throughout dinner, while they talked comfortably of books they had read, people they admired and other safe topics, she continued to examine her own feelings for some clue as to where her relationship with Mikhail might be headed.

Wryly, she remembered her father's teasing comment that she was the only one of his children who relished the careful analysis of a problem, pulling it apart into tiny pieces before meticulously arriving at a solution. That characteristic, which had sometimes made her seem slow and plodding compared to her more impulsive siblings, had stood her in good stead in her career.

A large measure of her success as a journalist stemmed from her ability to thoroughly analyze complicated situations and report her findings in terms other people could readily understand. But now, as she attempted to do that to herself, she was discovering that some human experiences didn't yield easily to such dissection.

"You're very far away," Mikhail said gently. "What is on your mind?"

Disconcerted yet again by his perceptiveness, Erin tried to evade the question. "Oh, I was just thinking about my family back in Wyoming. We're so different in some ways, and yet we manage to be very close."

"Do you miss being with them?"

"A little. . . . Not as much as I expected." She smiled. "You make it very hard for me to miss anyone."

"Good, that is as it should be." He put down his wineglass and gazed at her over the flickering candles. "I see the worry in you, Erin, and I wish there was something I could say or do to soothe it. But I can't, because the future is as hidden to me as it is to you. We will have to discover it together."

His admission that he too was uncertain of where their relationship was heading should have worried her, but instead she was reassured to know that he wasn't playing some sort of sophisticated game in which she would ultimately be the loser. As he had said, they'd come to each other honestly. Whatever happened between them would at least have that much going for it.

She slept that night in his arms after long, exquisite lovemaking that left her at once completely drained and utterly fulfilled. She deliberately refused to think about what lay ahead of her the following morning when she had to begin work on the assignment from Derek. All her considerable skill as a journalist would be needed to write objectively about the man who enthralled her body and soul. Her commitment to her profession demanded that she at least try, even as she doubted what chance, if any, she had of succeeding.

# Chapter Eleven

So how's the article going?" Jenny asked as she dropped a stack of mail on Erin's desk.

Looking up from the pages of what was supposed to be a final draft, Erin grimaced. "Okay, I guess. I'm not really sure."

"That doesn't sound like you. Is something wrong?"

Something . . . everything . . . Erin wasn't clear which. But she did know that the article wasn't turning out as she had expected. It was supposed to be a straight news story providing in-depth details on Mikhail's experiences in the prison camp, his charges of oppression by the authorities of his country and his adaptation to his new home. So far, so good. But other elements had crept in that added a level of perception that she couldn't help but recognize as intensely personal.

For almost a week she had wrestled with the problem of keeping her own feelings out of her writing, but the task had proved far more difficult than she could ever have envisioned. Over and over she thought she had finally gotten it right, only to go back and discover that what she believed was straightforward journalism was, on closer reading, nothing of the kind.

And yet the story was good. Better, perhaps, than anything else she had ever written. It had taken her a long time to come around to admitting that, principally because it meant that she should quit trying to make it into something it clearly wasn't going to be and send it through to Derek as it was.

Only the thought of how he would react made her hesitate. "Nothing's really wrong," she said slowly as Jenny continued to study her with concern. "It's just that the story has turned out to be less a clear-cut case of reporting and more a subjective look at how oppression can bring out extraordinary human characteristics."

"That sounds great," the younger girl insisted loyally. "Why should you be worried about it?"

"Because . . . the story should only be about Mikhail. But it isn't. Somehow a lot of myself got mixed in, and I don't know how to get it out."

"I'm not sure I understand. Isn't there bound to be something of yourself in anything you write?"

"Yes . . ." Erin admitted hesitantly. "But not like this." She couldn't quite go so far as to explain that what she heard in the words she had written was even more of a revelation to her than it would be to the general reader. It was as though a hitherto unacknowledged part of herself was speaking from the pages.

The days spent going over his experiences with Mikhail and the nights spent in his arms had coalesced into a single vision of him as a man in whom intrinsic human vulnerability coexisted with incredible strength and intelligence.

Her work on the article had led her to review all the acclaimed "Demertov Papers," which had first spurred her interest in him. Mikhail's writing brought home to her more forcefully than ever the depth of his talent as a writer and his determination to redeem brutalizing experiences by giving them meaning.

What stood out most remarkably in both his own work and the vision of him her article revealed was his remarkable lack of hatred. Despite all that had happened to him, Mikhail nurtured a genuine love and sympathy for the rest of the human race. He didn't in any way attempt to excuse the oppression he had suffered, but he brought it down to a human scale, so that both the victim and the perpetrator were seen struggling with their own fears and inadequacies.

The result was that readers could not merely sympathize with the person who appeared to be on the side of good. They were also forced to understand the motivations of evil and to feel the capacity for similar abuses within themselves.

His sensitivity to subtleties of human behavior and thought was so great as to make her confront a similar, though not yet as well-defined, ability in herself. Through the long, difficult hours she had spent at her typewriter a single truth had emerged to stare at her from the pages of her article and ring in every word she had written: She was in love with Mikhail.

Not merely infatuated, not merely overcome by admiration or enveloped in physical rapture. Love, pure and undeniable, shone in every phrase and image she had created. It soared beyond the confines of her subject to add an astonishing degree of insight and wisdom to what was no longer simply a profile of a man, but an affirmation of the age-old struggle to discover and attain the furthest limits of human potential, no matter how perilous the task.

The revelation of her true feelings at once frightened and elated her. No longer could she puzzle over why she had cast off the teachings of a lifetime to rush into intimacy with him. The intensity of her love was such as to make it unthinkable that it should be denied so fundamental a form of expression. But neither could she find consolation in the thought that if they weren't able to weave a lasting relationship, she could resume her old life without more than lingering regret, because that simply wasn't true.

In fact, she was almost unbearably defenseless against a degree of pain she could hardly even imagine, and her vulnerability was growing more intense with each passing hour. Though it seemed impossible, her very ability to love appeared to be increasing. A vast reservoir of emotion was opening up within her—in which she might easily drown.

"Erin . . ." Jenny said softly, "are you all right? You're so pale and you look almost . . . scared."

"What? Oh, no, I'm fine." Jerking herself back from her painful thoughts, she managed to smile shakily. "I was just wondering how Derek will react when he reads this." She gestured toward the pile of pages covered with scribbled rewrites that more often than not were themselves crossed out as she decided that the original version was best. "After I retype it, of course."

"I'll do that for you, if you like," Jenny offered. "I'm not really busy right now."

Touched by the offer, since typing reporters' copy wasn't one of the younger woman's usual responsibilities, Erin nonetheless shook her head. "Thanks, but I'll bet you're anxious to get out of here. Going anywhere special for New Year's?"

Jenny smiled, her eyes bright with anticipation of the night ahead. "No, my boyfriend and I are just going to stay at his place and split a bottle of champagne. I know that doesn't sound very glamorous, but I'm really looking forward to it."

"I don't blame you. I've never liked going out on New Year's, and tonight's no exception."

"Even though you're invited to Mr. Kent's party?" Jenny asked, her eyes widening as she envisioned the dozens of well-known, glamorous socialites who would be gathering at the managing editor's Fifth Avenue apartment.

"Even though. I just hope Mikhail enjoys it."

"Oh, that's right, he's going with you." Jenny couldn't quite keep a note of envy out of her voice, though she quickly explained, "I'm crazy about my boyfriend, and I wouldn't trade him in for anyone, but I've got to admit, when Mr. Demertov was up here the other day he really wowed me. I never knew anybody could be so—" Words failing her, she fell back on a tried-and-truism. "—so dreamy. He actually gives me goosebumps!"

Erin knew the feeling, although she was careful not to say so. The speculative looks that had come her way recently hadn't escaped her notice. She was fully aware that those of her co-workers who knew where Mikhail was staying were curious about the exact nature of their relationship. So far, at least, she had managed to keep them guessing, but she had no confidence that such a state of affairs could be maintained, especially after her article began to circulate.

An hour later she had typed a clean version of it, tucked it into an envelope and dropped it off on Derek's desk. Firmly putting aside her doubts about the wisdom of what she had done, she headed home to dress for the party.

As she unlocked the door she could hear the steady tapping of Mikhail's typewriter, the same sound that had filled the apartment through every waking hour of the last week except for those times when they were talking, eating or otherwise engaged.

Her own awareness of the difficulties a writer faced when beginning a new project prevented her from asking what he was working on, but she couldn't deny her curiosity. The first book or article or whatever he did in his new country was bound to excite even greater interest than his work ordinarily received. Would he continue the type of writing he had done in the past, or would this new work signal a departure as radically different as the new life in which he found himself?

Mulling over those questions, she stripped off the mahogany slacks and yellow-gold sweater she had worn to work and stepped under the shower. Memories of certain passionate interludes spent in similar circumstances flashed through her mind as she soaped herself with jasmine-scented lather and shampooed her hair. Though she struggled to keep her mind on the present, she was nonetheless hard pressed not to give in to the temptation to climb out, wrap a towel around herself and go interrupt Mikhail in a way he would undoubtedly appreciate.

Only the knowledge that she had barely an hour to get ready for the party kept her from doing so. Sighing, she dried off, cleared the mist from the mirror and tackled the problem of what to do with her face.

Not that it was much of a challenge. She radiated the sense of a supremely satisfied woman. It could be seen in the fresh glow of her apricot-tinted skin, the bright gleam of her emerald eyes and the graceful carriage of her slender body. Even her hair seemed unusually cooperative. After it was dried, she had only to put it up on hot rollers for a few minutes before brushing it into a flatteringly soft style that framed her face before falling in an auburn cloud to her shoulders.

Checking the time, she wondered if she should remind Mikhail about the party. The sound of the shower running in the guest bathroom told her it wasn't necessary. She suspected that he was looking forward to the event more than he cared to admit and resolved to do her utmost to make it a success, if only for him.

In front of her closet, dressed only in delicate lace undergarments and silk stockings held up by a matching lace garter belt, she studied the gown she had bought especially for the occasion. Now that she had admitted the full extent of her love for Mikhail, she could recognize its powerful influence in many of her recent actions. The turquoise taffeta dress was a vast departure from the rest of her wardrobe. It was an unabashedly sensual and romantic creation that a woman would wear only for a man she wanted very much to attract.

After strapping on the delicate evening slippers that matched it, she stepped into the gown. The full, ankle-length skirt rustled luxuriously. Above the narrow waist, the low-cut bodice revealed the swell of her breasts, while the equally scanty back framed the delicate lines of her shoulder blades. Wide, puffed sleeves and a ruffled collar that framed her face gave the final touch to the utterly feminine confection.

She added a spray of perfume in which rare flowers and spices mingled provocatively, then carefully secured the locket that Mikhail had given her around her neck. Suspended on a thin gold chain, it nestled in the shadowy cleft between her breasts.

Staring at herself in the mirror, she battled a final moment of doubt. Granted, it was a gala evening when a woman could be expected to dress rather more flamboyantly than usual. But she would be mingling with at least a few of her co-workers, most notably Derek himself, who might well guess the reason for such a dramatic transformation.

Even as she debated the merits of sacrificing vanity to good sense, the opportunity to change disappeared. Mikhail stuck his head into the bedroom and started to say something, then stopped stock still as he took in her appearance. The sudden flare of desire in his silvery eyes was reward enough for all her efforts even before he whistled softly.

"You have always been beautiful, Erin, but tonight . . ." Taking her hand, he turned her so that he could take in the full effect of the gown and the slender but ripely curved body it more or less covered.

A blatantly proprietarial gleam sharpened his gaze. "You look like a glorious butterfly. Every man at the party tonight will be drawn to you. But don't get any ideas about flitting around, because I intend to keep you close beside me."

That was fine with Erin, who couldn't deny a tiny spurt of pleasure at his possessiveness. Granted, it wasn't exactly in keeping with her view of herself as an independent woman, but the truth was that it could still be quite pleasant.

"You should talk," she teased, letting her gaze wander over him. "I'll have to fight the other women off with a big stick."

Though the words were said jokingly, she was only half kidding. Dressed in a black velvet evening suit and white silk shirt, he looked at once utterly elegant and ruthlessly masculine.

The costly materials and meticulous tailoring in no way softened the hard sweep of his shoulders and chest or the sinewy line of his narrow hips and powerful thighs. His golden hair, still faintly damp from the shower he had just taken, was brushed back from his broad forehead. Beneath slanting brows his eyes glittered dangerously.

The burnished skin pulled tautly over the almost harsh planes and angles of his face only emphasized his faintly predatory air. He looked like exactly what he was: a supremely fit male animal made all the more formidable by acute intelligence and unshakable determination.

It was difficult to remember that he was the same man she had laughed and joked with over the last few days and in whose arms she had discovered ecstasy beyond imagining, a man whose every touch was enticingly gentle. A slight shiver ran through her as she considered what a formidable enemy he would make. Toughened by merciless circumstances, he would be unlikely to grant the least quarter to anyone he felt deserved his condemnation.

The thought faded almost the same instant that it occurred as Mikhail reached for her gently. The hands on her shoulders as he held her coat were warm and enticing. Not for the first time she wished they were staying home with the whole evening in which to indulge the passion she knew was fully awake in them both.

But duty called, along with a reluctance to deny Mikhail what might turn out to be a very enjoyable excursion into society. He was certain to be the center of attention, even at a party crowded by luminaries in politics, entertainment, business and the media. But when she said as much on the way into the elevator, he merely laughed.

"Why would those people be interested in me? Even if some of them have actually read my work, as opposed to simply buying it, I'm sure they have far more engrossing concerns."

"Perhaps, but I still think you should prepare to be mobbed. Frankly, I doubt Derek would have invited me to this shindig on my own. He only did it because he knew I'd bring you along. You're quite a social feather in his cap."

Holding the taxi door open for her, Mikhail shook his head bemusedly. "You lost me. What is a *shindig?*"

"Sorry. It's a fancy party where people tend to put on airs."

"Okay, now, about the feather in a cap. That's Yankee Doodle, right? And—what is it—macaroni?"

Suspecting that she was being teased, Erin laughed. "Well, no, not exactly."

"Oh, yes, that much I know. I even know how the song goes." To her delight and the enjoyment of the taxi driver, who promptly joined in, he launched into a rendition of all the choruses to "Yankee Doodle" that lasted until they pulled up in front of Derek Kent's luxurious East Side apartment house.

As they got out the driver leaned forward to grin at them both. "That was great, Mac, especially those last few stanzas. I never heard them before."

Mikhail leaned forward, a conspiratorial gleam in his eyes. "I made them up, but don't tell anyone." Adding a generous tip to the fare, he grinned at the bemused man, took Erin by the arm and informed her sternly, "Stop giggling. If you're going to be seen with a literary lion, you should at least endeavor to look properly impressed."

"Oh, but I am," she told him between chuckles. "And I'm sure everyone else will be, too, particularly if you have a few more songs, especially bawdy ones, in your repertoire."

"At least a dozen, but unfortunately, most of them are in various East European languages, and I doubt this evening's guests would be able to appreciate them. I could, of course, endeavor to translate, but somehow, that just isn't the same."

"Don't worry. By midnight everyone will be so plastered you could sing the originals and they'd think they understood every word."

"Getting plastered is a New Year's tradition, isn't it?"

"For some." She smiled up at him engagingly. "I,

however, have plans for a rather private celebration once we escape from this one. And for that, I intend to stay relatively sober."

Mikhail's answering grin made it clear that he was in full accord. They were still smiling at each other when a butler in black tie and tails opened the door to Derek's apartment.

# Chapter Twelve

ℋer experience as a reporter had prepared Erin to mingle comfortably with all sorts of people, so she felt no self-consciousness as the butler took her coat and she and Mikhail strolled into the crowd of elegantly dressed men and women who exuded an almost palpable aura of wealth and power.

Her customary equanimity was quickly dented when she realized that not only was Mikhail an immediate source of interest and excitement, but that she was receiving a considerable share of attention herself.

The men's perusal was unmistakably appreciative, the women's less so. Whatever its origins, such scrutiny made her uncomfortable. She was glad for the solid strength of Mikhail's arm beneath her hand and the comfort of his nearness.

"What did I tell you?" he growled. "I'll be fighting off would-be interlopers all night."

The prospect didn't seem to particularly displease him. In fact, he might almost have been looking forward to it. A flicker of dismay coursed through her as she realized how much the man at her side relished a challenge.

She wasn't sure how she felt about inadvertently providing him with such a diversion, but she was certain that she was not going to stand by and let anything happen that she could prevent, so when Derek approached them there was a decidedly frosty gleam in her eyes, which the managing editor didn't miss.

"Erin, my dear," he murmured as he took her hand and coolly lifted it to his lips, "you should have warned me. Over the years I've managed to get used to the delectable vision you present in the office. But this—" his gaze ran over her body beneath the turquoise gown "—is quite another matter." Leaning closer, he added, "How is it that, after I've known you so long, you still manage to surprise me?"

Before she could respond, Mikhail interjected smoothly, "Is there any reason why she shouldn't? After all, I believe this is the first time you and Erin have had occasion to be in the same place outside of working hours."

Not quite masking the displeasure behind a jovial

smile, Derek murmured, "Is that a fact? How remiss of me. I must make sure such a lapse isn't repeated." Taking advantage of the duties of a good host, he remained with them as other guests began to filter over, all eager to be introduced to Mikhail. The men were honest in their respect for his courage, but the women found other qualities to admire.

Erin had to stand by politely as he was positively fawned over by a bevy of blondes, brunettes and redheads whose numbers grew with each passing moment. Worse yet, Mikhail clearly enjoyed their attention. He was completely relaxed and at ease. The combination of his devastating good looks, obvious affluence and innate sensuality brought out the hunting instinct in more than a few of the young ladies clustered about him. Erin found herself maneuvered farther and farther away, until at last she could just make out the top of his head above the crowd.

A low chuckle made her turn abruptly. Derek was lounging against one of the French windows leading onto the terrace garden. His thick chestnut hair was slightly mussed and there was a dull flush in his cheeks.

"Feeling abandoned, my dear?"

"No, of course not. I was just . . . looking for somewhere to sit down."

"To the best of my knowledge the bedrooms are still unoccupied. But somehow I don't think you'd go for that."

Erin stared at him frostily. "You're right." She

moved to pass him, only to find him blocking her way. Getting a firm grip on her temper, she murmured, "Excuse me."

Instead of stepping aside as she had hoped, Derek reached for her. Too late she realized that he had been drinking more than she had guessed, and also that the reflexes that had served him so well in professional football were still surprisingly intact. Holding her wrist, he drew her inexorably toward him. Short of making an all out scene, Erin had no choice but to comply.

When they were standing so close that she could feel the warmth emanating from his body and smell the Scotch on his breath, he muttered, "Demertov's a fool to let anything distract him from you. But you can't blame the poor fool for having his head turned by all the attention. After what he's been through, he must think he's died and gone to heaven."

He chuckled humorlessly. The sound made her emerald eyes darken with worry. Not only was he perilously close to being drunk, he was also furiously angry. "I waited too long with you, didn't I?" he demanded. "I should have put more pressure on you to go out with me instead of letting you dart away every time I got too close."

A grim smile twisted his mouth. "You know what stopped me? Something really funny. You're too damned good at your job. I didn't want to lose you, and I couldn't help but respect your ability." Dully, he shook his head. "Respect and beautiful women don't mix. I should have forgotten all about that terrific brain you've got tucked under all that gorgeous hair and just followed my instincts. If I had, you'd be in my bed now instead of Demertov's."

Even as she felt the embarrassed flush staining her cheeks, Erin fought to keep her composure. Coolly she said, "You don't know anything about my relationship with Mikhail, so why pretend otherwise?"

Derek stared at her unblinkingly. "Don't I? Even if I hadn't suspected the two of you were lovers the day of the press conference, I would have realized it when I read your article. There's no mistaking how you feel about him, and you're not the kind of cold-blooded woman who could keep from expressing those emotions physically."

Erin's eyes had widened as she listened to him. In the back of her mind she had presumed that Derek wouldn't even see her article until the next day at the earliest. But instead he must have gone back to his office that afternoon and, finding it on his desk, decided to read it immediately.

Hardly breathing, she waited for him to tell her that what she had written was too subjective to count as journalism and would have to be scrapped. When he did speak his words were so far from what she was expecting that she could hardly credit them.

"Of course, you must already be aware that it's the best thing you've ever written. I knew you were good, but frankly, I never guessed you were capable of that kind of quality. Very few of us are." Almost as an afterthought, he added, "You'll get the cover, naturally, and we'll run the story with a full complement of photos. I suppose we'd better talk about your salary while we're at it, since we both know you can write your own ticket now. I'm not about to lose you to another publication just because I'm kicking myself for letting Demertov move in on what should have been strictly my own territory."

Torn between relief that he liked the article and anger at his presumption that she was some sort of prize in a male tug-of-war, Erin bristled. "Let's get something straight right now. Professionally, I'm pleased that you like my work, and I'll be happy to discuss terms for my staying with *Focus*. But personally, I couldn't care less what you think of me, and I don't appreciate your insinuations about my private life, much less this idea you seem to have that I'm up for grabs, by you or any other man. I suggest you get rid of that notion right away, or you can forget any chance of my continuing to work for you."

Derek stared at her for a long moment. His face reddened further, and an ugly gleam appeared in his eyes. Slowly he said, "I believe I've already mentioned your temper. Demertov doesn't seem to have managed to cool it down any. Maybe you need to be taken in hand by someone better equipped to manage you."

She was on the verge of an outraged exclamation when he reached behind him, pushed open the French door and, still holding onto her wrist, propelled her into the garden. A blast of icy air struck her. She shivered and tried to free herself from his grip, but unsuccessfully.

Her resistance seemed to fuel his anger. "Come on, Erin, don't play dumb with me. You know what the score is. Sure, I'll do a lot to keep you with *Focus* because you're a good reporter. But I'll do a hell of a lot more if you give me some personal reason to look after you."

Outrage, no matter how justified, had gotten her nowhere. She decided to try a different tack to put an end to the encounter before anything unforgivable happened.

"I'm not interested in being looked after, Derek— for any reason. I'm more than satisfied to be treated strictly as a competent professional." After pausing a moment to let that sink in, she added, "It's freezing out here. Let's go back inside before your guests start wondering where you've gone to."

Her very calmness seemed to take him aback. He had expected an angry confrontation that might have escalated to the point where he would have felt justified in taking physical measures to subdue her. Instead, she presented the voice of sweet reason, subtly reminding him of both his desire to maintain their working relationship and how potentially damaging the gossip would be, should the events in the garden become known.

But beneath all that was an undercurrent of sympathy and tolerance that surprised them both. Even as she told herself that she should be furiously angry at Derek, she couldn't muster more than mild annoyance. Mikhail so absorbed all her thoughts and emotions as to leave little room for anything else.

A month earlier, or even a week ago, she would have turned on the man holding her as if she were a spitting cat. Instead, she was prepared to forget the entire matter—as long as it ended quickly. Turning slightly, she urged Derek back toward the door.

The icy wind had begun to penetrate even the alcohol-induced fog enveloping his brain. Its sobering effect was evident in his rueful smile. Quietly he said, "You're one terrific lady, you know that? What's Demertov thinking of to let you get away?"

"Is that what I'm doing?"

The low, dangerously calm voice startled them both. Mikhail stood at the open door, his big body blocking their view of the party going on behind him. As though in slow motion, Erin took in every detail of his appearance. The hands that had always touched her so gently, but which she suspected could be brutal when he felt it was necessary, were clenched into fists at his sides. Despite the cold, his face was pale. A pulse beat near the curve of his jaw.

Derek was nothing if not realistic. Recognizing both the futility of what he had attempted to do and the immediate danger staring him in the face, he dropped Erin's wrist. She took a quick step forward, putting herself between the two men.

"I'm cold, Mikhail," she said softly. "Let's go back inside."

For a moment she thought he would refuse. Derek must have thought so, too, because he flexed slightly, preparing himself for the blow that might well be coming. The vision of the all-out brawl that would undoubtedly result spurred Erin to act.

Determinedly she took Mikhail's hand while sending Derek a radiant smile that made it impossible for anyone to believe that anything untoward had happened between them. "I know you never thought twice about playing football in all sorts of weather, but some of us aren't quite that hardy. Much as I appreciate hearing how much you like my article, I could stand to be a little warmer."

While rattling on about inconsequential things she managed to steer both men back inside the apartment. A few curious glances came their way, but the guests were enjoying themselves too much to be easily distracted. Derek allowed himself to be drawn off by a florid-face banker and the silver-haired anchorman of a network news show, who wanted him to settle an argument they were having about what teams were likely to make the Super Bowl.

Erin offered no protest when Mikhail put a firm arm around her waist and guided her in the direction of the study, where a cheerful fire was blazing. Sitting down close to it, she let the warmth seep through her gratefully. For long moments neither one of them spoke, until at last he said, "I looked up suddenly and you were gone. Why did you leave?"

"Leave?" she echoed, a spurt of indignation flaring in her. "I'd hardly describe it that way. You were too busy with your fan club to notice anything else. And I didn't feel like hanging around to watch you being fawned over."

"You were jealous," he said with sudden understanding. "That's what caused all this."

The pleased smile that banished the last of his anger only increased hers. "I was not," she insisted hotly. "I just thought it was ironic, after all your big talk about keeping me to yourself, that you didn't even realize I wasn't with you anymore."

Lowering himself beside her on the couch, Mikhail said quietly, "Oh, I noticed all right. And as soon as I could politely disentangle myself, I went looking for you." His voice hardened perceptively. "Imagine my surprise when I found you on the terrace with our host. Hardly the night for a moonlight stroll, is it?"

"We weren't strolling. We were just talking."

"What about?"

"Work." The skeptical arching of his eyebrows forced her to elaborate. "Derek had a little too much to drink, but he still wanted me to know that he liked the article I did on you. That's all."

"How very thoughtful. Couldn't he have waited until you were in the office?"

"Apparently not. Look, I really would prefer not to talk about him. I'm still cold, I could do with some food, and frankly, this is not shaping up to be the greatest New Year's Eve I've ever spent, so let's just drop the whole subject. All right?"

Mikhail stared at her for a long moment before he slowly nodded. "Stay here. I'll get us both something from the buffet while you get warm."

Rising, he touched a gentle hand to the gleaming mass of her hair, letting a soft auburn curl wrap itself around his finger. She couldn't repress a quiver of desire as his gaze captured hers. "If our host returns, I trust you will make it clear to him this time that you are otherwise engaged?"

Bewildered by her own acquiescence, Erin nonetheless nodded. She watched as he strolled away, mingling easily with the other guests, several of whom stopped him long enough to exchange a few words. Although he was too far away for her to hear what was being said, she was by no means oblivious to the sense of excitement and fascination he sparked. Even among such sophisticated, dynamic people, Mikhail stood out. It seemed as though everyone wanted to be seen with him, but some weren't satisfied simply with that. Erin stiffened when a particularly lovely blonde rested her hand on his arm, smiling up at him.

He made no immediate effort to escape her touch, but moments later he did move away, continuing toward the long rows of tables covered in white linen and loaded down with all manner of holiday delicacies. A lovely brunette in an amber silk gown cut low enough to make Erin's own décolletage look modest apparently asked him something about the caviar, which sparked yet another of his devastating smiles.

Unable to watch anymore, Erin turned away. She stared into the fire, fighting against the doubts and insecurities that were beginning to plague her. The long, hard hours she had spent working on the article had left her tired and on edge. She told herself that she was letting trivialities upset her.

Of course Mikhail was especially popular with the female guests. Why shouldn't he be? She was far too familiar with the overwhelming impact of his masculinity not to understand that other women would be similarly affected. That didn't mean she had anything to worry about.

Not for a moment did she doubt that he was an intrinsically honorable and decent man. Although the words had not yet been said, she was certain that he considered himself committed to her in a way that would transcend any attraction he might feel for another woman.

That being the case, why did she continue to be so unaccountably anxious and disheartened? On the verge of trying to discover the reason for her unease, she was forestalled by his sudden return. Carrying two large plates and accompanied by a waiter loaded down with an ice bucket, champagne bottle and two crystal goblets, he grinned at her engagingly.

"I hope you meant it when you said you were hungry."

Eyeing the more than ample selection of patés, meats, vegetables and pastries that he had chosen, she couldn't help but laugh. "If I wasn't, I would be now. That looks delicious."

The waiter opened the bottle for them, filled the tulip-shaped glasses, leaving room for the wine to breathe, and took his leave. The high-backed couch effectively screened them from the rest of the study and the rooms beyond. Snuggled close together, they shared choice tidbits while making slow but steady inroads on the champagne.

Erin put all thoughts of the scene in the garden and Mikhail's angry response firmly aside. In the relaxed, companionable way that they had shared from the beginning, they laughed and teased each other while talking about nothing in particular. Not until the strains of a waltz reached them did they leave their secluded corner, and even then, they didn't stray far.

Cradled in his arms, her head resting against the smooth velvet of his evening jacket, Erin gave herself up to the beauty of the music. They moved effortlessly together. His hand on her waist was warm and solid. The other caressed the bare expanse of her back, lingering at the particularly sensitive points that he already knew so well.

A low sigh of mingled contentment and need escaped her. Meeting his eyes, she smiled. The same sensations shone clearly in his silvery gaze. More than simply their bodies were in accord. Their very hearts and spirits seemed to float in perfect harmony.

They were still dancing when the sudden excitement of the crowd alerted them to the fact that the new year was about to arrive. Mikhail drew her into a shadowy corner of the room. The lights were turned out and a breathless hush descended, only to explode into cheers as the clock chimed midnight.

In the midst of blaring horns, popping champagne corks and laughing shouts, he captured her effortlessly in his arms. Cradling her head in a big, gentle hand, he kissed her long and deeply.

Enthralled by the taste, scent and feel of him, her senses whirled out of control. She was powerless to do anything other than respond fully with all the warmth and passion of her generous nature. Her breasts swelled against the rock-hard expanse of his chest, the nipples growing insistently taut and swollen. Her slender arms wrapped around him ardently, her fingers tangling in the thick gold of his hair.

As his tongue plunged insistently into the moist cavern of her mouth all the strength seemed to go out of her. Her legs trembled and might have given way if not for the steely strength of the arms that held her. She made no protest when he pressed her to him intimately, making her acutely aware that his need matched her own.

A sudden blast of music as the band swung into a new set drew them reluctantly back to earth. Oblivious to the amused looks of the guests closest to them and the resentful stares of a few who couldn't hide their envy at the sight of such transcending passion, they gazed at each other dazedly.

Mikhail had to take a deep breath before he could speak, and even then his voice was shaky. "Let's get out of here."

Erin nodded mutely. Every part of her was crying out in need. She couldn't bear to remain there, surrounded by other people, when all she wanted was to be alone with him. Moments later she stood wrapped in her coat just inside the lobby as the doorman flagged down a cab. When it pulled up to the curb, Mikhail helped her in before sliding in next to her and giving the driver their address.

They rode in silence without looking at each other. Once Erin glanced up to see the driver watching them with concern. She smiled faintly, guessing that he thought the couple in the back seat had argued and felt sorry for anyone starting the new year that way. If only he knew, she thought impishly. The sheer, overwhelming force of their desire compelled them to refrain from touching each other, even with their eyes, until they were safely hidden away from all the rest of the world.

Once they were inside the apartment, she deliberately delayed the moment of their coming together. After carefully hanging up her coat, she moved around the living room, pulling down shades, tidying a pile of magazines, even fluffing the pillows on the couch. She was just reaching for a file that needed to be returned to her briefcase when a bronzed hand closed gently but firmly around her wrist.

Mikhail had come up behind her so silently that she gasped. The sound was abruptly cut off as, without giving her a chance to protest, he led her purposefully down the corridor and into his bedroom. The room was dark, and there was a definite chill in the air. But that wasn't what caused Erin to tremble. It was the look in his eyes, the half-menacing, half-tender gaze of the fully aroused male that made the breath catch in her throat.

Unfastening his bow tie, he strode toward her. When only inches separated them, he muttered, "Take off that dress."

Startled, she stared up at him doubtfully. Was this apparently fierce determination, so far removed from the gentle, tender lover that she knew, some sort of joke?

Seeing her disbelief, Mikhail moved quickly to convince her that he was utterly serious. After tossing his jacket on the chair beside the bed, he began to unbutton his shirt as he said, "I am not teasing you, Erin. There's simply no way I can love you slowly and patiently tonight. I can't wait that long. So unless you want that very beautiful dress removed precipitously, I suggest you get out of it now."

Gulping, she realized that he meant what he said. It was on the tip of her tongue to object, to tell him that she wasn't about to be treated to any show of roughness, when she stopped herself. Mikhail wouldn't hurt her, she was certain of that. So why pretend that they didn't both want the same thing with equal urgency?

The zipper gave way smoothly beneath her quick tug. A shrug of her shoulders was all that was needed to send the dress slipping to the floor. The instant it fell, she realized that she had forgotten all about the silk stockings she was wearing and the lacy scrap of a garter belt that held them in place. Combined with her half-cup bra and tiny bikini panties, they gave her an alluringly sensual air that wasn't lost on Mikhail.

His eyes ran over her so hungrily that she felt almost scorched by them. The heavy gold cuff links he had just removed were dropped swiftly on the bedside table as he reached for her. Through the shirt that hung open to the waist she could see the bronzed skin of his massive chest, thickly covered with golden hair. The muscles of his powerful arms rippled sinuously against her softness.

"So beautiful . . ." he groaned, letting his callused palms run over her demandingly.

Erin trembled beneath his touch. Caught up in the waves of desire pounding through her, she was barely aware that he had insistently unclipped her bra and pulled it from her. The tiny clasps of the garter belt didn't yield as easily, and frustrated, he drew back slightly. Against her mouth he demanded, "It's sexy as hell, but take it off."

She did as he said, her eyes never leaving him as he swiftly unfastened his slacks and slipped out of them. His briefs followed immediately, leaving him a bronzed giant standing naked in the faint light filtering in from the hallway.

Erin forced herself to stand perfectly still as he approached her again. His big hands slid down the vulnerable line of her back and beneath the rim of her last garment to squeeze and knead her buttocks compellingly. Vividly aware of his strength and of the urgency of his desire, she cried out softly as he lifted her, and wrapped both her legs around his waist as he carried her to the bed.

Even as they fell onto it, he was stripping the fragile lace from her. He had said that he couldn't wait, and she believed him, so it came as a great shock when she realized that despite the strength of his need he was determined to ensure her own arousal.

His mouth was warm and gentle as it followed the slender line of her throat, his tongue darting out to taste the sweet hollow at the base of her collarbone before continuing on downward to the cleft separating her breasts, where his locket still rested. His fingers traced all the way around the delicately carved gold before stroking the fullness of her nipples.

"Mikhail . . . please . . ."

His only response was a low growl. She could feel the tremors wracking his powerful body as he strove to control his own passion while fueling hers. Not that any such effort was needed. She was already on fire for him, almost mindless from the currents of pleasure darting through her. When his mouth claimed the taut peak of her breast she moaned softly. Each swollen peak was tenderly suckled before at last his mouth drifted further down her body, lingering on the soft incline of her waist, the indentation of her naval and the flat plane of her abdomen.

Twisting beneath him, unable to endure much more, Erin cried out softly. Mikhail glanced up for a moment, his eyes locking with hers as he deliberately confirmed her surrender. When he moved again an instant later it was to bring them together with a shattering power that reached to the very depths of her soul.

Far away in the back of her mind she was conscious of an added element in their lovemaking that made it different from any that had gone before. It was as though Mikhail were deliberately sealing his possession of her, branding her as his own in a way that she would never be able to erase.

The power of his movements combined with the fiery tenderness of his restraint as he deliberately held himself back until her own pleasure crested, banishing any chance she might have had of resenting his actions. She could only yield totally, finding in absolute surrender a fulfillment beyond anything she could ever have imagined.

In the instant when the world dissolved around her in a blazing explosion of light and sound, Mikhail was with her fully. He cried her name deep into her mouth as his passion spent itself.

Clinging to each other, they slid almost instantly into sleep. Their bodies didn't fully separate, even through the long hours of the night, as they lay entangled in each other's arms, their breaths mingling as naturally as their dreams.

# Chapter Thirteen

It was still well before dawn when Erin awoke. She stirred reluctantly, unwilling to lose the delicious sense of well-being and security that filled her. Only gradually did her sleep-dazed mind clear sufficiently for her to acknowledge certain less serene feelings.

She was lying naked under the sheets, her body still half covered by Mikhail's long, hard length. One sinewy thigh was thrown over hers, and a bronzed hand rested near her breast. The soft sound of his breathing reverberated through her. Moving slightly, she gazed down at him.

A lock of golden hair fell across his forehead above eyes shielded by closed lids and inordinately thick lashes. His lips were slightly parted, the hard lines of his face relaxed. He looked utterly at peace and almost shockingly vulnerable.

All the vast love she felt for him welled up in her, and her hand moved lightly to trace the ridge of scar tissue on his back. A quiver of pain ran through her as she deliberately forced herself to think of all that he had suffered. His very survival was a miracle. That he had also emerged from what was truly hell on earth with his mind intact and his will unbroken was a rare testimony to the power of the human spirit.

In the days since they had become lovers she had carefully kept from thinking about how his experiences might have marked him. With his ready adaptation to his new life, his colloquial English and his obvious ability to successfully compete in the sophisticated world of the wealthy and powerful, it was very easy to think of him as someone who had always been on the winning side. But that was wrong. More than anyone else she had ever known, Mikhail was all too familiar with defeat, and even death.

How did he reconcile the extreme changes in circumstance that he had experienced over such a short period of time? Or did he even try? Wasn't it more reasonable to believe that he was simply existing from moment to moment until the shock of being lifted from one world to another eased somewhat and he was able to begin once more to think and plan?

And when that happened, when the inevitable day arrived and he was able to take a close look at his new surroundings and decide where he wanted to go from there, how would she fit into his thoughts? Would he feel compelled to remain with her because of the intimacy they had shared? Would the love that she felt for him become simply the walls of a new prison that in the end would be as bitterly hated as any he had known before?

Tears misted her emerald eyes as she forced herself to confront the doubts and insecurities that had finally begun to surface the night before at the party. She had no difficulty in recapturing the image of Mikhail surrounded by a crowd of beautiful, adoring women. Nor could she deny the fact that any number of them would be only too willing to take her place in his bed and his life. The stubborn pride that had carried her so far in her profession tempted her to do everything possible to keep him for herself. But did she have that right? Didn't simple human decency demand that he be allowed a choice?

After slipping out of bed she scooped up the clothes that lay discarded on the floor and padded down the hall to her own room. Moments later she was in the shower, scrubbing herself vigorously and trying hard not to think about the demands of her conscience.

Wrapped in a robe, her face free of makeup and her freshly washed hair hanging loosely around her shoulders, she was standing at the kitchen counter making coffee when Mikhail appeared. Despite the early morning chill he was wearing only pajama bottoms that rode low on his lean hips. He ran a hand absently through his rumpled hair as he smiled at her.

"How come you got up so early?"

Erin forced herself to look away, unwilling to be drawn yet again by the potent force of his attractiveness just when she most needed to keep a firm hold on herself.

"It isn't really. It just seems that way because we got to bed so late."

"Hmmm. . . ." He laughed softly, and his arms slipped round her waist to draw her back against him. "And it was much later than that when we finally fell asleep." His lips nuzzled the warm curve of her shoulder. "I can't remember the last time I slept so well."

"Me neither," Erin admitted, "but . . ."

"But what?" he murmured distractedly, his attention focused on the ultrasensitive nape of her neck, where he dropped feather-light kisses.

Twisting, she tried to elude his grasp, but he took her movements for playfulness and didn't release her. "M-Mikhail, please . . . I have a lot to do."

The serious, almost desperate, note in her voice reached him. His devastatingly gentle caresses stopped as he looked up, puzzled. "Erin, what is the matter?"

"Nothing. . . . I told you, I just have a lot to do."

It was more difficult than she could have imagined to meet his gaze as he studied her intently, but she managed to do so for long enough to convince him that she meant what she said. For a perilous moment she thought that he intended to press her for an explanation of her sudden withdrawal. When he didn't, she breathed a sigh of relief, even as she realized that the reprieve was only temporarily. Mikhail was far too perceptive not to sense the tension building within her, but apparently he was willing to wait at least a little while in the hope that she would reveal the cause voluntarily.

He let her go and poured two mugs of coffee as he asked, "So, what's all this urgent business you have to take care of?"

"Well, to start with, we . . . uh . . . have to take down the tree."

It sounded absurd even to her, but Erin held on to the excuse for dear life. She simply wasn't ready to talk to him yet, not before she had a chance to get her scattered thoughts in order.

"All right," he said at last, "but first perhaps we had both better get some clothes on."

Erin nodded, well aware of how difficult it was to stand so close to him without giving in to the temptation to ignore the dictates of her conscience and sink again into the radiant glow of pleasure that they had basked in the night before. At least when there were more layers of clothing between them, she might have a fighting chance of sticking to her resolve.

She took her coffee back to the bedroom and pulled a clean pair of jeans from the closet, along with a bulky sweater that fit her so loosely that she usually didn't bother to wear a bra with it. But, unwilling to dare fate any more than she could help, she deliberately put one on. After pulling her hair back in a ponytail she added a faint touch of lip gloss before returning to the living room.

Mikhail joined her a short time later, after showering and shaving. The utter relaxation she had noted in him earlier was gone, replaced by a wary watchfulness that tore at her heart. The last thing she wanted to do was to cause him pain for any reason, but she suspected that however carefully she phrased what was on her mind, he wasn't going to take it well.

In silence they stripped the ornaments from the tree and stored them carefully away in their boxes before removing the strands of lights. Mindful of the needles that were falling onto the rug, they tied the branches with cord before removing the tree from its stand. Erin held the door as Mikhail carried the tree out to the service elevator.

While he disposed of it downstairs she vacuumed up the needles and replaced the furniture in their accustomed places. There was always a certain sadness in throwing out the remains of a Christmas tree, but she had too much else on her mind to dwell on it. All it really meant to her was that the holiday was over and that everyday life was once again taking over.

By the time he returned, she was back in the kitchen, fixing breakfast. Mikhail joined her there, but didn't speak until they were seated at the table. In between bites of ham omelets and cranberry muffins they talked about the party, recent news events, anything other than what was uppermost in both their minds.

He had cleared away the dishes and started another pot of coffee before at last he said, "Erin, I think you will admit that I am generally a patient man." A faint gleam shone in his eyes as they both remembered that he had been anything but the night before. Ruefully he admitted, "But you strain my endurance to the limit. Please tell me what has happened to the warm, loving woman I held in my arms only a few hours ago."

Now that the moment was upon her, she was hard pressed not to retreat. Only the undeniable knowledge of how much he meant to her, and of how much more important his happiness was to her than her own, gave her the courage to face him.

"Nothing's happened to me," she said softly, "except that I've been doing some thinking, and I've finally reached some conclusions we have to talk about."

Mikhail nodded curtly, but said nothing, as they took their coffee into the living room and settled down in front of the cold fireplace. Erin curled up on the couch as far away from him as she could get, aware of what her body language was telling him but unable to prevent the silent communication that made him frown.

Realizing that the situation was only going to get worse the more she delayed, she took a deep breath. "Mikhail, last night at the party . . . when I saw you with all those other people . . . I realized that ever since you got here you've had almost no opportunity to get out and make new acquaintances . . . to begin building a new life for yourself without interference from anyone else."

He opened his mouth to interrupt, but she went on hastily. "Interference, even when it's perfectly well meant, can do you a lot of harm. I can't really imagine how I would feel in your place, but I'm sure that I'd be very vulnerable to being . . . taken over by someone who might not even realize what was happening, but who could still prevent me from building other relationships that might really be better for me."

"What on earth are you talking about . . . ?"

"Please, let me finish. What I'm trying to say is that even though you've come to . . . mean a great deal to me, and even though I want more than anything to believe that we can have a future together, I'm afraid that unless you have a chance to consider alternatives you'll mistake gratitude for love and end up feeling trapped and resentful. I just couldn't . . . bear that. . . ."

Her voice broke. She had to duck her head to keep him from seeing the sudden tears that threatened to spill from her eyes. For a woman who had always prided herself on being able to control her emotions under even the most trying circumstances, she was having remarkably little success maintaining even the slightest degree of detachment.

The utterly feminine part of her that had come to

the fore in recent days was putting up a fierce struggle against the facade of calmness she was struggling desperately to maintain. Instincts she had paid very little attention to until Mikhail brought them vividly to life were demanding that she stop such nonsense at once and enjoy whatever he was willing to give no matter what the reason.

But she couldn't do that: not because she wasn't tempted—the urge to do so was all but irresistible—but because she would have to live with herself afterward, and with the knowledge that she had violated her own fundamental principles out of purely selfish motives.

Yet even the knowledge of how guilty she would feel might not have been enough to stop her had it not been for the single, overriding fact of her love for him. For the first time in her life she truly understood what love between a man and a woman really meant. Because of it she could put Mikhail's well-being ahead of her own, knowing even as she did so that, however painful the outcome, she would never regret having done so.

Forcing herself to look at him, she said as calmly as possible, "What I'm trying to say is that, before our relationship goes any further, I think you should give yourself the opportunity to meet other women and get to know them. It's not impossible that you may find you don't really feel for me the way you think you do. You might even discover that you . . . care for someone else more. . . ."

She stopped, unable to go any further. Her fingers were clenched around her coffee mug so tightly that they ached, but she didn't notice. The hurt welling up in her heart blocked out everything else.

Mikhail was staring at her in genuine confusion. He shook his head bewilderedly. "I don't think I understand what you're saying. . . . You want me to go out with other women?"

"Y-yes. . . ."

"To date them?"

"Yes."

"Perhaps take them to bed?"

Erin bit her lip so hard that she tasted blood. Her voice was little more than a whisper as she said, "You seem to have gotten the idea. Surely it isn't necessary to go over all the details?"

"Indulge me. After all, I'm a novice at this sort of thing and frankly, I feel as though you just yanked my feet right out from under me."

His sarcasm drilled through her with razor sharpness. Wincing, she murmured, "You know perfectly well I've never been involved in anything like this . . . overwhelming either. It's cruel to suggest otherwise."

"But it isn't cruel of you to suggest you want to break off our relationship?"

"That's not what I said! I just want you to have a choice. . . ."

Mikhail's eyes flashed dangerously. He stood up, then strode over to the fireplace to stare into it silently. The rigid line of his back warned her that he was growing angrier by the moment. When he turned to her again his hands were jammed into the pockets of his jeans, and he was scowling heavily.

"I would never have imagined you were capable of this, Erin. You seemed far too honest to play such callous games."

Baffled, she shook her head. "I'm not . . . I don't understand what you're saying."

"I'm saying this whole charade wasn't necessary! If you wanted to break off with me, you had only to say so. I'm not claiming I would have liked it, but at least I would not have lost respect for you, as I have now."

Unable to believe what she was hearing, Erin rose shakily. "You must have misunderstood me. All I'm saying is that I'm concerned about you and your feelings. I'm not playing any sort of game!"

"Aren't you?" he sneered. "I really missed the whole point of that episode on the terrace, didn't I? I actually believed there was nothing to it."

"There wasn't! Mikhail, please, you aren't making any sense."

"On the contrary, this is the most sensible I've been since I first set eyes on you. When I think how easily you affected me . . ."

He broke off, turning away again as though he couldn't bear the sight of her. Grimly he demanded, "Last night, when we got home, did you decide you were in the mood for a farewell performance, Erin? A little something to tide you over until Kent could step in?"

"That's disgusting! What on earth is happening to you? You're twisting everything I've said and done."

Angrier than she had ever been before in her life,

Erin grabbed hold of his shoulder, trying to force him to face her. "I'm not going to listen to that kind of talk from anyone, no matter how much I l—no matter what."

The icy look in his eyes when he finally deigned to look at her made her throat clench. Whatever was going through his mind, it was very ugly and very dangerous. She had only to meet his gaze to realize that.

In the back of her mind she remembered the image that she'd had of him that first evening at the airport. He had appeared to her then as an immensely proud, fierce man who, no matter how weakened and hurt, would still be capable of exacting a full measure of revenge from those he considered his enemies.

Since then that initial impression had been overlaid by far gentler, more tender memories. She had temporarily lost sight of the remorseless strength of his character until his anger was suddenly turned against her.

Too late, she realized the battle he was waging to hold on to some remnant of his self-control. His powerful hands lashed out to seize her arms, not holding her painfully, but so firmly that she had no hope of escape.

"Don't worry, Erin," he growled when he saw the spark of fear in her eyes. "You won't have to listen to me much longer. There is very little more I wish to say to you, except that I hope you do not discover that the payment for your story was too steep.

Undoubtedly Kent will reward you far more generously. But then, you will at least be going to him with enough experience to be able to please a man."

His hands tightened for just a moment, almost but not quite enough to leave bruises. "Don't say it," he warned as she opened her mouth to attempt a last, desperate denial of his accusations. "I cannot be sure how I will react if I have to listen to more of your lies. Why I thought you were different is beyond me. I should have realized it wasn't possible for you to have come to care for me as deeply as you seemed to in such a short time."

He laughed bitterly, the sound echoing the pain stamped on his hard features. "I thought I had learned some difficult lessons in the past, but this is by far the worst. However, at least you have been kind enough to point out exactly how I might console myself."

Letting her go so abruptly that she had to catch hold of the mantel to keep from falling, he stalked away toward the guest room. Over his shoulder he said, "Be assured I intend to take your advice. I have no doubt several of the lovely ladies I met yesterday evening will be able to appreciate my company, despite how quickly you have tired of it."

Behind him Erin slumped against the couch, her eyes wide and dazed. Instinctively she wrapped her arms around herself in a futile effort to stop the trembling that threatened to shake her body apart. The full enormity of his suspicion and anger overwhelmed her. She couldn't make the slightest sound in her own defense, nor was she willing to try.

In her grief-stricken state she saw only one explanation for Mikhail's behavior. He could never have felt for her as she did for him, or he would never have been able to turn on her so totally and with such vile accusations.

Unable to move, she was barely aware of the sounds from the bedroom or of his sudden return. Not until he was standing in front of her, fully dressed and with his duffel bag once more slung over his shoulder, did she manage to look up.

"The rest of my things will be out of here by tomorrow."

She continued to stare dazedly at him, hoping against hope that the angry apparition in front of her would vanish and in its place would be the gentle, caring man she had come to know.

But the lover she had cherished was gone without a trace. There was nothing left but a cruel, hurting stranger whose very words tore at her heart. And then he was gone too, vanishing out the front door without a single backward look.

A slow, trembling breath escaped her. She was distantly aware that she was behaving like the victim of a traumatic accident. Shock was settling in, leaving her mercifully numb. She barely made it to the couch before all the strength went out of her. For uncounted hours she remained there, oblivious to the hot trickling of tears down her ashen cheeks.

Only when the dim winter light had faded and the room was bathed in darkness did sensation begin to return, and with it came pain beyond anything she had ever known.

# Chapter Fourteen

$\mathcal{M}$ r. Kent wants to see you," Jenny said softly, her eyes dark with concern as she surveyed the pale, quiet young woman sitting at the desk. The first week of the new year was supposed to be filled with renewed energy and purpose, but Erin clearly lacked both. Jenny had never seen her so downhearted. She looked almost . . . breakable.

"Right away, I suppose," Erin murmured, glancing up from the article she had been diligently trying to read for the last hour. The neat lines of type kept dissolving in front of her eyes to be replaced by the image of Mikhail's face, stiff with anger and bitter accusation.

"No, actually, he just said you should stop by

whenever you had a moment." Though she tried, Jenny couldn't keep the surprise from her voice. She had never seen the managing editor in such a quiet, almost subdued mood. Even Sheila was unable to explain the sudden change from his usual brash, demanding self.

That startling statement reached Erin even through the anguished haze that had enveloped her from the moment when Mikhail had walked out of her apartment and her life. Absently she said, "Is Derek all right?"

"Uh . . . I'm not sure. . . . Sheila thinks he may be coming down with the flu or something. He's been so quiet."

A slight frown appeared above Erin's darkly shadowed emerald eyes. "That doesn't sound like him. Maybe Sheila's right."

"Well, anyway, whether he's sick or not, he'd like to see you."

Erin shrugged. She closed the folder, then stood up and pulled on her suit jacket, though it didn't quite disguise the new fragility of her form. Her face was pale, the almost-translucent skin drawn tautly over her delicate bones. Deep shadows were visible beneath her eyes, despite her efforts to hide them with makeup.

Sheila smiled tentatively when Erin entered the managing editor's outer office, and one look was enough to worry her. "Is everything okay?" she asked softly.

Erin forced herself to smile reassuringly. She

could barely confront the shambles of her relationship with Mikhail in her own mind. Talking about it would make it real in a way she could not yet endure. "Of course, or it will be, once I find out what our great leader wants."

Sheila took the hint and went off to announce Erin's arrival. Erin sat down on one of the Ultrasuede couches positioned around the room and tried to concentrate on a magazine. Since there was no set time for her appointment, she expected to wait. But the secretary came back at once to show her in before carefully closing the door and returning to her desk.

Derek was in his usual spot behind the marble-top table, his jacket off and his shirt sleeves rolled up. He looked tired, and beneath his perpetual tan his face was almost wan. A spark of concern ran through Erin even as she told herself that she had no reason to be solicitous of him after the stunt he had pulled at the party. But try as she might, she couldn't blame him for precipitating the confrontation with Mikhail. If their relationship had been all that it should have, nothing he had said or done would have had any effect.

Settled across from him in one of the visitor's chairs, she waited for Derek to explain the summons to his office. The delay struck her as unlike him. She was used to a barrage of instructions, questions and complaints with—on very rare occasions—a grudging compliment tossed in.

When he finally spoke, after scrutinizing her thoroughly, his voice was low and hesitant. "Are you feeling all right, Hennessey? You look like hell."

For the first time in days some remnant of spirit stirred within her. "Thanks a lot. That's just what I needed to hear this morning."

Derek managed a faint grin, not up to standard, but still somehow reassuring. "Now, don't get your Irish up. I just don't want one of my star reporters coming down with something when I'm about to give her a new assignment."

Perking up slightly, Erin tried to show at least a flicker of interest, but without much success.

"Don't overwhelm me with enthusiasm," Derek muttered. "I couldn't take it this morning."

Despite her resolve not to be concerned about him, she caught herself murmuring, "Speaking of coming down with something, you don't look all that great yourself."

"So what if I don't? You should be delighted to see me laid low."

Erin's eyes widened slightly. Implicit in his tone was the suggestion that her pleasure would be justified. Was he actually admitting that he had behaved badly?

"Look," she said slowly, "if you're talking about what happened at the party, just put it out of your mind. I'm certainly not going to mention it to anyone."

Derek grimaced. With an effort he met her eyes. "I never thought you would. But I still want you to know I'm sorry. You didn't deserve to be put on the spot like that."

The last thing Erin had expected from her brash, self-assured editor was an apology. It took her a moment to come to grips with it. "Consider it forgotten, okay?"

He nodded gratefully. "Thanks, but just one more thing. If I caused trouble for you with Demertov, I'll do whatever I can to patch it up. Maybe I should talk to him, or . . ."

"No! That isn't necessary. You didn't cause anything."

Derek looked at her doubtfully. "I'm relieved to hear it. Then you two are getting along fine?"

"Uh . . . well . . ."

"That's what I thought." He shook his head ruefully. "I would never have pegged you for the kind who could be brought down by a man, Hennessey. Where's that old Irish spirit?"

"I think it went back to the emerald isle," Erin muttered noncommittally. Though she was genuinely over whatever anger she had felt toward Derek, she still wasn't prepared to discuss her personal problems with him.

He sensed her reluctance, and with a surprising degree of tact he changed the subject. "We were talking about your new assignment."

Desperate for something to distract her from her anguished thoughts, she would have welcomed any absorbing task. But the one Derek offered astounded her.

"Do you remember a few months ago when you drew up an outline for a series of stories about the various international organizations affiliated with the

U.N., what they're supposed to be doing and what, if anything, they actually accomplish?"

Erin nodded silently. She had no trouble recalling the outline, or the fact that Derek had found the idea interesting, while doubting her ability to carry it through. He had seemed inclined to give the assignment to one of the senior political reporters, and she had reconciled herself with poor grace to that inevitability.

"I want you to get started on it right away so that we can begin running it in the first February issue."

"What made you change your mind?"

The blunt question was answered in kind. "Your coverage of Demertov. That convinced me that you're capable of the type of sustained effort and perceptive analysis this assignment will require. Plus the fact that, while you were always a good writer, you seem to have crossed over the barrier that separates the good from the outstanding."

Erin swallowed hard, more moved by his praise than she cared to admit. "Thanks, Derek," she said softly. "At least something worthwhile came out of it all."

He shrugged off her appreciation. "I figure I owe you one. Now that we're even again, I can be as tough on you as ever."

She couldn't help but laugh. "That's good. If you'd kept on being so mild and reasonable, none of us would have known what to make of you."

"Had you stumped, huh?"

"I'm afraid so. Crusty, hard-nosed editors aren't supposed to suddenly turn into softies."

"Don't worry, I'm sure I'll be back to normal in no time."

"That's good . . . I think," Erin teased. She got up to go, feeling far more kindly disposed toward him than she had when she came in. His apology had made her realize that people were rarely as easy to predict as they might seem. Granted, Derek would probably always have a broad streak of self-centeredness in his nature, but at least he was occasionally able to temper it with consideration for others.

She had no illusions that he would have given her the assignment simply to make peace between them, but neither did she doubt that he had put some effort into thinking of a concrete way to express his regret, rather than merely passing it off with words. While nothing could erase her abiding sorrow over Mikhail, Derek's thoughtfulness had at least let a little ray of light into her life.

Some of the customary energy and excitement she felt when tackling any new project were making themselves felt as she went back to her office to immerse herself in the assignment.

By midafternoon she had set up several appointments and was busy bringing together essential background information from the magazine's archives. Caught up as she was in the familiar hum of activity, she didn't notice Sheila's arrival in her small office until the secretary coughed politely.

"Things seem to be getting back to normal around here," the other woman said. "You're pounding away at the typewriter, and our glorious leader is once more snapping and growling at everyone."

Erin grinned, pleased to hear that Derek's brief bout of conscience wasn't being unduly extended. "If you've come down here to hide out, be prepared to help. I've got a ton of information to plow through."

"Far be it from me to get between a reporter and her backgrounding. I just came to add these to the pile." She dropped a handful of folders on top of a precariously balanced stack. "Derek thought these might be helpful."

"Translation: He wants to make sure I won't overlook the points covered in them."

"Right in one. Now, on to more serious matters. Am I correct in thinking that you have a particular fondness for pre–Colombian art?"

"It's my single most expensive weakness," Erin admitted dryly.

"Good, because Sidney and I have tickets to a preview of the new show that's opening at the Fiske Gallery. Want to go?"

"Do I ever. It's being billed as the finest collection of pre–Colombian art ever assembled outside Latin America. Dare I ask how Sidney got added to the guest list?"

"Who knows? With the triple life my dear husband leads as a would-be actor, part-time model and possibly the most popular substitute teacher in the city's high schools, he's liable to have come up with the tickets anywhere. He wants to go because there's some big deal producer who's planning to attend. I'm going to protect him from the fairer sex, since they have a distressing habit of drooling all over him. Somebody really ought to come with us who's actually interested in art."

Sheila's offhand explanation didn't fool Erin. Beneath both their stunningly attractive exteriors, she and the improbably named Sidney were warm, thoughtful people. He had probably accepted the tickets just so they could get her out for a few hours and cheer her up.

It would have been almost as tactless to reveal that she had seen through their ploy as to refuse the invitation. Gratefully Erin accepted. She dreaded the thought of another evening alone at home, when not even her new assignment would be able to keep her heartache at bay.

Leaving the office shortly after five o'clock, she opted to walk uptown to her apartment. The weather was cold, but she was warmly dressed in a cashmere wraparound coat and lined boots. Enveloped by the stream of people emerging from the buildings, she let herself be carried along. For once the anonymity of the city was welcome. The crowd absorbed her without a flicker of interest. Automatically matching its fast pace, she kept her mind resolutely blank as exercise soothed away some measure of her tension.

By the time she got home, she was actually feeling relaxed and looking forward to the show. After changing quickly into a simple ankle-length black sheath she coiled the heavy weight of her hair into a neat chignon at the nape of her neck, freshened her makeup and, as a finishing touch, sprayed on her favorite perfume.

The results weren't bad. Considering how poorly she had slept in the last few days and how little she had eaten, she looked better than she had any right to. Vast quantities of tears had left her eyes with a luminescent glow. Her face was pale, but that only emphasized the purity of her complexion. Even the air of fragility that she couldn't hide made her seem softer and more delicate.

Telling herself that she could take a certain pride in being able to so effectively mask the emotional turmoil seething inside her, she went downstairs to wait for Sheila and Sidney.

They arrived moments later, pulling up in the bright yellow Edsel that was Sidney's pride and joy. He had found the car in a junkyard some ten years before and spent a good part of the decade restoring it to its former glory. Now that the model had become something of a status symbol, he'd turned down numerous offers to buy it for impressive amounts of money. Sidney was nothing if not stalwart in his affections. Only Sheila counted for more with him than his Edsel.

"Hop in," he invited as the traffic behind him began to blare in protest.

Sliding in beside Sheila, Erin was quickly caught up in the couple's cheerful chatter about the day's events. Sidney had been on a shoot for a dog-food commercial. He regaled them with descriptions of the petulant collies who had refused to eat even in the face of dire threats to their lives.

"I keep telling my agent I'm the soulful, indoor type, but he keeps getting me jobs where I have to look rugged and put up with animals. Last time it was a pinto pony I swear was out for blood. I couldn't sit down for a week."

"Serves you right for looking like you do," Sheila informed him unsympathetically. "If you would only gain thirty pounds and lose some hair people would take you seriously."

"I doubt it," Sidney griped. "Whenever I open my mouth to say something even half-way intelligent, I get the feeling I'm really shocking everyone. Just the other day I got lavishly complimented for being so articulate."

"What's wrong with that?" Erin asked.

"I was ordering lunch at the time." Stentorially he intoned, "Gimme a pastrami on rye, hold the mustard, and a cola to go."

Laughing, they pulled into a garage, where Sidney negotiated briefly to make sure the Edsel would be treated with proper respect. That task completed, he offered an arm to each lady. "Shall we?"

The gallery was already crowded, but a quick glance around was enough to tell Erin that she was one of the few people there who was actually interested in the exhibit. The rest had come to see and be seen. Many of the same faces she had noticed at Derek's party were once again in evidence. Or at least it seemed that way. After a while all the beautiful people began to look somewhat alike.

Leaving Sheila and Sidney chatting with the producer he had wanted to meet, Erin wandered off to enjoy the artwork. The evocative textures and colors of the pottery absorbed her so completely that she lost all awareness of her surroundings. The sights and sounds of the party faded away, becoming no more than a blurred backdrop.

Part of her pleasure in the exhibit came from the awareness that she was actually enjoying herself. That was a victory of sorts. Though she wasn't so foolish as to believe she would ever be able to get over Mikhail, at least she was still capable of appreciating the beauty of the world beyond the darkened limits of her own life.

Content to remain on her own in the midst of the preening, posturing crowd, she wandered along the fringes of the large room. The attentive looks of several men who would have liked to make her acquaintance passed her by completely. Her very lack of interest spurred their curiosity, but she remained oblivious to her own impact. She thought of nothing but the exhibit, until a prickling at the back of her neck distracted her and she turned to find Mikhail standing near the gallery entrance, staring at her.

He was dressed once again in evening clothes that emphasized the rugged masculinity of his build and the golden virility of his chiseled features. To Erin it was impossible to believe that any man had ever

215

looked more desirable. But she still couldn't help but note that his burnished skin was pulled even more tautly than usual over his high-boned cheeks and that his face looked slightly drawn, as though he hadn't been sleeping or eating well.

With him was a lovely young blond woman who she vaguely remembered from the New Year's party. Muffy somebody or other. Tall and slim, she had the elegantly cool beauty of an aristocrat. The deceptively simple white dress she wore looked almost demure, until she moved. Then it parted at the sides to reveal slender, tanned legs clear to the thigh.

As she gazed up at Mikhail Erin's throat tightened. For just a moment she allowed herself to meet the hard glitter of his silvery eyes. The mingled pain and pleasure she saw there startled her. He seemed glad to see her, but reluctant to admit as much, even to himself.

In the next instant any softness she thought she had glimpsed in him vanished. His expression became shuttered, revealing nothing. Puzzled as to what could have caused the sudden change, it took her a moment to realize that Sidney had come up behind her.

Even to somebody who knew him as well as she did, he was breathtakingly handsome. His movie-star good looks, combined with obvious intelligence and self-deprecating humor, set him apart in any crowd. As he smiled at her she was aware of several women standing nearby who were torn between the urge to drink in the sight of so much sheer male splendor and the need to shoot daggers at the innocent object of his attention.

"Sheila and I are about to tackle the buffet," he said. "How about joining us?"

Standing across the room, Mikhail couldn't make out his words, but he was clearly conscious of the friendly warmth underlying the exchange. Erin glanced back at him in time to see the stiffening of his broad shoulders and the anger that flitted briefly across his face before his expression became coldly contemptuous.

Fully aware of how he had misinterpreted the situation, Erin was torn between rage at the unfairness of his judgment and an obstinate determination that he not see how much he had hurt her.

Beaming a smile at Sidney that could have melted an iceberg, she took his arm, turned her back on Mikhail and walked away.

# Chapter Fifteen

"I'm in the mood for Japanese food today," Derek said. "Is that okay with you?"

Erin nodded absently. It didn't make any difference to her what sort of restaurant they went to for the usual once-a-month lunch the managing editor felt compelled to have with each member of his staff. She doubted that she would be eating much anyway.

In the week since her unexpected encounter with Mikhail at the gallery, any hope she had cherished that time would ease her anguish had evaporated. Far from lessening the sorrow she felt, each day seemed to bring only further reminders of how much she loved him and how empty her life was without him.

The restaurant was just around the corner from

*Focus*'s offices. Erin had been there several times before and had always enjoyed the subdued ambiance and excellent food, but that afternoon she was barely aware of either.

Settled at a table near the window with a platter of Derek's favorite sushi in front of them, she made a valiant effort to throw off her dejection. The weather had turned unexpectedly warm, giving New Yorkers a brief respite from winter. Her work on the U.N. articles was going very well, so much so that she was tentatively planning a quick trip back to Wyoming to visit her folks. Her latest paycheck had reflected her new, considerably increased salary. She had promptly gone out and spent it on clothes in a futile effort to cheer herself up.

The violet wool suit and warm-pink silk blouse were part of the booty from that shopping expedition. Vibrant colors and the judicious use of makeup went a long way toward camouflaging the paleness of her complexion and the shadows under her emerald eyes, but they didn't entirely manage to fool Derek.

"Is it the new series that's keeping you up late these days, Hennessey, or have you just decided you can do without sleep?"

Erin sighed, well aware that there was no good answer to that. If she claimed to be working late every night she would be giving the impression that the assignment was too much for her to handle. If she admitted the truth, that she deliberately avoided going to bed until she was ready to drop, she would be opening the door to personal questions that she wanted desperately to avoid.

Reluctantly she said, "A bit of both, I suppose. The series is going very well, but it's also very absorbing. I lose track of the time."

Derek looked unconvinced, but apparently decided not to pursue the subject. Gesturing with his chopsticks at a particularly succulent slice of raw tuna set on a bed of vinegared rice, he said, "Why don't you try that, and while you're at it, have a beer. It wouldn't hurt you to start gaining back those pounds you've been losing."

Accepting the tidbit, which was delicious, she shrugged. "Isn't there a saying that a woman can never be too rich or too thin?"

Derek snorted derisively. "You can bet no man ever believed the second part." There was an unaccustomedly gentle light in his eye as he added, "I could point out that you're a damn good-looking woman who didn't need to lose an ounce, but since we've agreed our relationship is strictly professional, I won't."

Erin's eyes widened slightly. "You were in your high school or college debating club, weren't you?"

About to take a swallow of his beer, Derek froze. He glanced around quickly to make sure no one was listening. "Now how in hell did you figure that out?"

"Because there's a name for what you just did, mentioning something by saying you're not going to. I forget what it is, but it's an old debating technique everyone learns—*if* he belongs to a debating club." Smiling slightly, she asked, "So how come everyone thinks you did nothing but play football until you took that sportscasting job that led eventually to *Focus?*"

"Because that's what I want them to think. It's a lot easier for me to deal with the pseudo-intellectual types I encounter in this job if they think I'm strictly a dumb jock."

Delighted by her discovery, Erin couldn't resist the urge to pry a bit further. "You didn't by any chance work for your school newspaper, did you?"

"What if I did?" Derek growled, obviously chagrined at having been found out.

Taking pity on him, she relented slightly. "Don't worry, your secret is safe with me."

"It's a good thing I already know you can keep your mouth shut or you could find yourself *Focus*'s stringer in Bora Bora."

"Didn't any of those management books you're so fond of tell you not to threaten sensitive, creative types like me?"

"Actually, they never mentioned anyone like you," he shot back. "I'm convinced you're an original. Now, eat your sushi."

Grinning, she did as he said. Her appetite remained nonexistent, but the beautifully prepared Japanese food was such a treat that she couldn't resist it. They had started on their second platter of seafood when Derek asked, "Any problems with the series so far?"

"Some, but nothing I can't handle. A few of the agency heads aren't too happy about being interviewed, but they're astute enough to realize what it will look like if we run a story without their comments. One or two have tried to turn it into a public relations coup for them. That didn't continue past the point where they realized that I had done my homework and had a pretty fair idea of what they were trying to conceal. Since then, everything's been moving along fairly smoothly."

"Good. So we can still plan to take the first story to press in a couple of weeks?"

"I don't see why not."

Satisfied, Derek nodded. He waved over the kimono-clad waitress so he could order a plate of tempura and more beers. When she was gone, he leaned back in his chair and surveyed Erin quietly.

"There's something else we need to talk about."

The sudden somberness of his tone warned her that she wasn't going to like what he had to say. She was right.

"It's about Demertov."

Quickly Erin said, "I don't want to discuss him."

"Maybe not, but I still want you to hear what I have to say."

She started to shake her head, but was stopped by Derek's stern look. "This is strictly business," he insisted. "I'm not asking what went wrong between the two of you personally. I just want you to be aware that a twist has cropped up that may affect how he's viewed by both the media and the public."

Against her will she was driven to ask, "What twist?"

With maddening slowness Derek took time out to

taste the tempura after it was placed before him. He grinned approvingly at the waitress before continuing. "On second thought the whole thing is just a rumor, so maybe I shouldn't say anything."

"You can't do that," Erin protested. "Out with it!"

"If you insist. . . . It seems that a French newspaper, one that's admittedly very leftist, has turned up a report to the effect that when Mikhail was in prison he collaborated with the authorities against his fellow inmates and members of the opposition underground. Supposedly that's the real reason why they eventually let him out and why he seems none the worse off, despite all the horrors he supposedly endured. Furthermore, they're also going to charge that he was in fact a double agent, working for the C.I.A. at the same time as he was cooperating with his own government. Covering his bets, so to speak."

Shock darkened Erin's eyes to sea-green pools. Her stomach clenched tightly as all the color fled from her face, only to return an instant later in full fury. "That's absurd! No one could believe such a lie! I know how much he suffered. I've seen the scars. . . ."

She broke off, embarrassed. It made no difference that Derek was certainly aware of her intimate relationship with Mikhail. She still wasn't comfortable talking about it.

Tactfully ignoring her comment, he said, "It really makes no difference whether the charge is true or not. Unless it's countered, it could do him a great deal of harm."

Erin took a deep breath, fighting to get control of herself. All the mental and emotional barriers she had carefully erected to keep from thinking about Mikhail crumbled in an instant. The thought that he might be unjustly charged, held up to false accusations, threatened with public condemnation, was unbearable.

"It isn't fair," she murmured, afraid to speak above a whisper lest her outrage break free. "He lived through a year of absolute hell, and before that he was constantly on the run, never knowing what would happen from one day to the next. He had no chance for a family life, children, any of the things we all take for granted. Yet he persevered. He never gave up on himself or his beliefs. It's contemptible for anyone to suggest otherwise."

Derek listened to her patiently. Not until she had run out of breath and was once again silent did he say quietly, "You really think a lot of the guy, don't you?"

Unable to deny it, she nodded. Her eyes were bright with unshed tears. "There has to be some way to prevent that story from being taken seriously."

He shrugged doubtfully. "I suppose there might be. . . ."

Erin wasn't fooled by his hesitation. She knew him too well not to realize that he would never have mentioned the problem unless he had at least some idea of how to solve it. Schooling herself to patience, she waited for him to reveal it.

"To start with, Demertov has to be told, so he can prepare to rebut the charges, but there's nothing I can do," Derek explained slowly, "simply because I doubt that he would believe anything I said. On the other hand, he might be inclined to listen to you. . . ."

"Me? I'm the last person he'd believe."

"Oh? Why's that?"

"Because he thinks . . . that is . . ." Erin broke off. She wasn't about to burden Derek with the full story of what had happened after the party. "Never mind. I just don't think he'd pay attention to anything I said."

"That's too bad," Derek said regretfully. "Then I guess there's nothing we can do."

"You could get in touch with his publisher," she suggested. "Tell him what's going on and leave it up to him to tell Mikhail."

"No way! If you think I'm about to leak a story that far, you're crazy. I'm not even sure telling you was ethical. I only did it because I think Demertov deserves a break."

Stymied, Erin fell silent. She tried to come up with another alternative, but every plan she thought of had some intrinsic flaw. Finally she had to admit defeat. "All right, maybe I am the only person to tell him. But I still can't."

"Why not?"

"Because I don't even know where he's living."

Her boss grinned unsympathetically. "So what? You're a reporter, aren't you? Put that well-honed investigative ability to work. I bet you'll have his address by this afternoon."

Erin wasn't anywhere near as confident, but she wasn't about to admit that. Back in her office half an hour later, she shut the door and began making phone calls. Her first try was Mikhail's editor. The woman listened politely to her explanation of who she was and what she wanted, but absolutely refused to comply.

"I'm sorry, Ms. Hennessey, but I cannot release Mr. Demertov's address to anyone. I wouldn't do so with any author, but in his case security is a particular concern. I'm sure you understand."

Erin did, reluctantly. She hung up and called Mikhail's agent. There the response was even firmer. "Not a chance. If you want to leave a message for him with me, I'd be glad to relay it. But that's the best I can do."

It wasn't good enough. The message could get lost or Mikhail might simply choose to ignore it. Precious hours, even days, could be lost while she waited to hear from him. Combing through her files on him, she tried futilely to come up with another lead. Nothing. He simply hadn't had enough of a chance to put down roots yet. A check with her contact at the credit bureau confirmed that all his charge cards carried the address of his publisher. The stores she knew he had shopped at had already delivered all his purchases and been paid in full. They had no reason to know his current whereabouts. Calls to the top hotels in town turned up the fact that he had spent several nights at one of them after leaving her apartment, but he had checked out the week before and left no forwarding address.

In exasperation she finally called Derek. After explaining the problem she said, "There was a blonde at your New Year's party. Tall, slender . . ."

He chuckled. "There were at least a dozen of them."

"No, this one was different. I'm pretty sure she's not a model or an actress. She's beautiful enough for either, but she seems a little too aloof for that. My guess is she comes from money, probably serves on charity committees, that sort of thing. I think I heard someone call her Muffy."

"Melinda Trina Bradshaw," he said instantly. "She hates to be called Muffy. Hasn't answered to it since she was twelve. Very old money and very good legs. What about her?"

"I saw her the other night with Mikhail at a gallery. So maybe if I could get in touch with her, she would know where he is."

Derek didn't seem any happier than she was about the beautiful blond socialite dating Mikhail, but he was able to provide the young lady's address and phone number.

Erin took a break before trying to reach her. Sipping a tepid cup of coffee, she made a deliberate effort to get control of her wayward thoughts and emotions. Pride demanded that she give no hint of how deeply she loved Mikhail and how hurt she was by his involvement with another woman.

When she was certain that she could manage at least a semblance of professional detachment, she picked up the phone again. Ms. Bradshaw, her housekeeper announced, did happen to be at home. If Erin would wait a moment, she would tell her who was calling.

The warm, cheerful voice that promptly came on the line was a surprise. Whatever else she was, Melinda Trina Bradshaw was at least not overly taken with herself. She listened to Erin courteously before she said, "Yes, I do know where Mikhail is living. Ordinarily I wouldn't dream of giving anyone's address out, but in this case . . ." She hesitated a moment before asking, "Are you by any chance the person Mikhail was living with when he first arrived here?"

Erin's stomach fluttered. Despite her careful preparations she couldn't keep a tremor from her voice. "Y-yes . . . I am. . . ."

"I thought you might be. Hold on a sec and I'll get his address."

It made no sense that, having learned of her true role in Mikhail's life, Melinda was willing to give her information that she would otherwise have withheld. But that was exactly what she intended to do.

After the socialite read off a street number in a nearby neighborhood on the Upper East Side, Erin tried to thank her, but the woman brushed that aside. "It must be my New England upbringing. I can't stand to see something good go to waste. Whatever the problem is, I hope you two work it out."

So did Erin, more than she could admit, even to

herself. Her spirited defense of him had forced her to remember all that he had endured. After what he had been through he was bound to expect disappointment and betrayal at every turn. It was up to her to convince him otherwise, if only belatedly.

But that was easier said than done. Tired out after the hectic day, and not feeling at all at her best, she wasn't ready yet to confront him. First she went home, stripped off her clothes and stood under the shower long enough to feel somewhat revived.

After blow-drying her hair she dressed in pleated tan wool slacks that were gathered at the waist and a creamy silk blouse. The outfit was casual but elegant. She looked very good, but it wasn't obvious that she had taken great pains with her appearance.

Leaving her hair brushed loosely around her shoulders, she redid her makeup to hide the dark shadows under her eyes and put a hint of color in her cheeks. A spray of her favorite perfume was the final touch to boost her confidence. With a quick glance at herself in the mirror, she tossed on her camel's-hair coat and left the apartment quickly, before she could have any second thoughts.

The taxi ride to Mikhail's place seemed endless, but finally she arrived in front of an elegant East Side town house. After paying the driver she got out and stood on the sidewalk, trying to get up the courage to ring the bell. It occurred to her that he might be out or, worse yet, not alone. She really should have called first. But it was too late to think of that. Winter darkness was rapidly closing in. A chill wind blew off the river, piercing through even her warm clothes. Shivering, she made up her mind.

Her heart was beating uncomfortably fast and her stomach tightened painfully as she pressed the door bell.

# Chapter Sixteen

The chimes sounded deep within the town house, reverberating hollowly. Erin waited through long, seemingly endless moments, straining to hear any hint of approaching footsteps. Nothing. Stubbornly she rang the bell again. After another indeterminate delay she reluctantly acknowledged that Mikhail was not at home.

At a loss as to what to do next, she surveyed the rapidly emptying street. The unusually warm weather of the afternoon was gone, replaced by a bitter cold that cut to the bone. She was tired, hungry and growing steadily more anxious. Common sense told her to leave and try to reach him the next day, but such reasonable behavior was impossible in light of her feelings for him.

He had to come back sooner or later. Deciding that it wouldn't hurt to wait a bit longer, she pulled her coat more snugly around her and turned up the collar against the wind. The entrance to the town house was slightly recessed behind a stone overhang. It provided a small amount of shelter, but not much.

Half an hour passed, and it got colder and damper. Her feet, shod only in high-heeled pumps since the day had seemed too warm to require boots, were beginning to turn numb. She found a scarf in her purse and put it on, all the while mentally rehearsing what she should say to him.

A policeman strolled by on his beat. He glanced at her carefully, and she tried to look as though she were waiting for a bus. Something about her must have reassured him, because he didn't bother her.

Erin glanced at her watch. Seven o'clock. Sensible people were at home having dinner. Her own stomach growled, but she ignored it. Pacing back and forth, she tried to get some feeling back into her feet. Her fingers were becoming stiff, but a search through the pockets of her coat revealed that she had forgotten her gloves.

Seven thirty. Maybe he had gone out somewhere . . . with someone. Maybe he wouldn't be back for hours, or perhaps not even until the next day. She was an idiot to be standing there on a dark, deserted street, inviting all sorts of trouble. If she weren't completely crazy she would go home.

She stayed. The policeman came back. He was a young man, very pleasant, but very firm.

"Are you waiting for someone, miss?"

"Yes," she answered quietly, not taking offense at what was, after all, simply his job. "I'm hoping the man who lives in this house will be coming back soon. It's very important that I talk with him."

"You picked a bad night for it."

She grimaced. "It was so warm earlier that I didn't expect this." Without even realizing that she was doing so, she began automatically to draw him out, just as she would on an interview. "But I suppose you're used to cold. Have you been walking a beat long?"

He shook his head wryly. "Only a couple of months, though it seems longer." They fell to talking about the city, the changes they had seen in the last few years, the good points and the bad. It occurred to Erin that she wasn't the only one asking questions. With a few well-placed inquiries the young policeman managed to determine that she was unlikely to have any nefarious object behind her vigil.

"I'd better be going," he said regretfully. They had shared a simple human exchange that for a short time, at least, had broken through the barriers of their solitude. Turning to leave, he added, "I hope you're not planning to stay here much longer. It looks as though we're in for some rain."

Erin glanced up at the sky in dismay. He was right. Leaden clouds obscured the topmost floors of nearby office towers. Even as she watched, scattered drops began to fall, splattering against her forehead and running down the bridge of her nose.

*"Oh, great!"* Muttering, she brushed it aside and retreated back under the stone overhang. Maybe it would be content to just drizzle.

It wasn't. Within minutes the first few drops had become a downpour. It rained so hard that the water bounced back off the pavement, soaking her shoes and the cuffs of her slacks. It was just as well that she could no longer feel her feet, Erin thought glumly, since they were sopping wet. Too bad the rest of her hadn't turned numb. She was only too aware of the sodden weight of her scarf and coat clinging to her body, the wet tendrils of hair plastered to her forehead, the icy fingers of water sliding beneath her collar to trickle down her back.

No matter how she tried, it was impossible to keep the rain off. The wind blew it at her almost horizontally, making the stone overhang useless. She tried to keep her spirits up by telling herself that it could be worse, it could be snow. But that didn't work very well. She was wet, cold, miserable and feeling more like a full-fledged idiot with each passing second.

But she still couldn't bring herself to leave. Some hitherto unsuspected streak of do-or-die stubbornness forced her to stay. Not simply because of what she had to tell Mikhail, but because she couldn't bear the thought of walking away, perhaps only moments before he returned. She badly needed to see him, to be close to him, even if his terrible anger hadn't eased at all.

Shaking her head ruefully at such singlemindedness, she peered through the rain-swept gloom, trying to see if anyone was coming. Of course not. Nobody, absolutely nobody but she, was outside. In the entire city of almost eight million people everybody else was snug and dry, well-fed and content. Everybody, including Mikhail, who was undoubtedly comfortably ensconced in some restaurant or—she flinched at the thought—some lovely lady's apartment.

Or was he? A familiar figure had turned the corner near the town house, walking, head bent, into the rain. Even obscured as he was by the darkness and the sheets of water, there was no mistaking the big body clad only in slacks, a turtleneck sweater and a tweed jacket. His shoulders were hunched and his hands were jammed deep into his pockets. In the glare of a streetlight she could make out the burnished gold of his hair clinging wetly to his head.

Her throat tightened convulsively. In another moment he would see her, and she still had no idea what she intended to say to him.

Not that it mattered. The moment their eyes met, all ability for rational thought fled. She couldn't move or speak, could only wait as the disbelief she saw in his gaze gave way slowly to something that looked very much like the first faint stirrings of hope.

"Erin . . . ? What are you doing here? Standing out in the rain like this . . . why . . . ?"

"I need to talk to you," she said, surprised that she managed to sound calm when everything inside her was exploding with an almost painful combination of pleasure and fear. It was so good, so right, to be with him again that she forced herself to put aside her doubts about what he really thought of her sudden appearance on his doorstep. "Could we go inside?"

He hesitated for just a moment, still struggling to come to terms with her presence. When her tentative question finally registered he nodded quickly. "Yes, of course. You must be soaked."

"So are you," she pointed out rather unnecessarily as he unlocked the door and stood aside to let her in. They were both dripping water onto the wood parquet floor, but Mikhail didn't seem to mind. He was too busy staring at her.

"You're really here. . . . I thought perhaps I was just imagining things."

Startled, she looked up at him. It was perfectly believable that she might call up his presence out of her heated thoughts, but for him to do so . . .

Seeing the surprise in her eyes, he laughed dryly. "It wouldn't be the first time. I seem to have encountered you everywhere in the last few weeks."

"I-I don't understand. . . ."

He shrugged, looking away. "Let's get dried off first. Then we'll talk."

Erin had to agree. The puddle forming at their feet added nothing to the decor. Not that there was much to it to begin with. The entry hall was bare of furniture, as were the spacious living room and the dining room, which smelled of fresh paint. A few cartons were scattered around, with several more piled near the marble staircase that led to the second floor.

The house had the vaguely forsaken air of a place that has been empty for a long time, but that couldn't detract from its old-world elegance or the gracefulness of interiors well suited to another, more genteel age. She could easily understand why Mikhail would choose such a home for himself.

Touching her arm lightly, he said, "There are towels upstairs, and I should be able to find a robe for you."

About to tell him that wasn't necessary, Erin thought better of it. Her clothes were sticking soggily to her, and she felt chilled clear through. Besides, it was ridiculous to hesitate about facing him in only a robe when he was accustomed to seeing her in far less.

They parted at the top of the stairs, he to what she guessed was the master suite overlooking the back of the house and she to the guest room he indicated. Some of its furniture had already arrived and been put in place. A large brass bed covered by a vibrant star-pattern quilt was framed on either side by low pine tables topped in marble. A golden oak wardrobe took up most of one wall, near the door leading to the bathroom.

Erin had taken off her coat and shoes and put both in the shower to drip when Mikhail knocked. He handed her a pile of fluffy white towels and a navy-blue cashmere robe. For just an instant she thought she saw his quicksilver eyes flicker with concern as he surveyed her bedraggled form. But his tone was no warmer than any conscientious host's as he said, "You should get out of those things before you catch a chill."

She thanked him quietly, but waited until the door was closed behind him and she heard him walk away before attempting to undo the buttons of her blouse. Her stiff fingers were awkward, and she was trembling so badly that it was an effort just to stand upright. She hadn't counted on the shattering effect his presence would have on her. Being alone with him in the silent house forced her to confront the full intensity of her love. She desperately wanted to go to him at once, convince him that he had no reason to mistrust her, and find both forgetfulness and rebirth in his arms.

Only her pride stopped her. She had no confidence that he wouldn't rebuff her. It would be the height of foolishness for her to misinterpret what was only a simple act of courtesy from an innately gracious man. Just because he had allowed her into his home, it didn't follow that he was willing to reassess their personal relationship and admit that his accusations had been unjust.

When she was finally able to unfasten her blouse, she hung it up in the bathroom, along with her slacks. Even her lingerie was wet. After a moment's hesitation she took it off as well, toweled herself dry and put on the robe.

A glance in the mirror made her grimace. The dark-blue cashmere hung on her slender body. All her makeup was washed off, and her hair hung in tendrils to her shoulders. The paleness of her skin made her emerald eyes look enormous. She had the fragile, uncertain air of a waif.

And there didn't seem to be much she could do about it. The hair dryer she found in a cabinet under the sink helped a little. But nothing could disguise the vulnerable quality of her mouth or the anxious pulse beating in the alabaster column of her throat.

Reluctantly admitting that she had done everything possible to restore her appearance, she padded across the bedroom and gingerly opened the door to the hall. There was no sign of Mikhail, but from downstairs she caught a whiff of a wood fire and the distant sounds of someone moving around in a kitchen.

The steps of the marble staircase were cold beneath her bare feet. She moved down them hastily, not slowing until she reached the bottom. A sudden burst of wind rattling against the windows made her tense. The rain seemed to be getting worse. She peered out at it worriedly, wondering if she would be able to get a cab when it was time to leave.

A soft sigh escaped her. If only things were different. If only the closeness that had existed between them so briefly hadn't been destroyed by bitterness and anger. How wonderful it would be to spend that night and every night with him upstairs in his bed. No storm that raged outside would be able to equal the tempest of their passion.

Erin bit her lip hard as she felt her cheeks grow hot and flushed. Why was she tormenting herself with such thoughts? They could achieve nothing and would only make it even harder for her to face him.

Determinedly forcing her mind back to the reason for her presence, she headed for the kitchen.

At some point in its long life the house must have undergone extensive remodeling that had transformed the entire rear of the first floor into a combination cooking, dining and living area. Dark-gold terrazzo tiles lined the floor beneath white stucco walls and a pressed copper ceiling. A huge brick fireplace stood in one corner, the source of the wood smoke Erin had sniffed. In front of it were a comfortable overstuffed couch and several tables. Nearby a large trestle table and chairs sat under a brass and pewter chandelier. The silver bowl of dried fall flowers on the table picked up the red, yellow and blue shades of the hand-painted tiles decorating the kitchen.

Ordinarily she would have been too distracted by such a delightful room to notice much of anything else. But as it was, the interior details barely registered. All her attention was focused on the man standing at the kitchen counter, preparing a pot of coffee.

Mikhail was wearing only the terry-cloth robe she had seen so often from across the breakfast table. His golden hair was tousled, as though it had been roughly toweled dry. The broad sweep of his shoulders and chest tapering down to his slender waist, narrow hips and long, powerful legs made her breath catch. She remembered all too vividly the feel of his lean, hard body against her own and the havoc he so easily wreaked within her.

Feeling absurdly exposed despite the robe that covered her from below her fingertips almost to her ankles, she had to fight the urge to flee back upstairs. How had she ever imagined that she could face him calmly, without revealing the torrent of love and sorrow he had caused? The mere sight of him was almost enough to make her forget why she had gone there in the first place.

Almost, but not quite. Remembering the accusations that were about to be unleashed against him, she forced down her fears. It was imperative that they talk, no matter what the consequences for herself. An instant later he became aware of her presence and looked up, and she was able to meet his gaze calmly.

"Do you need any help with that?" Erin asked.

He shook his head, his eyes wandering over her slender, vulnerable form. "No, thank you. Why don't you sit down by the fire? It should be warm over there by now."

Erin did as he suggested. Curled up on the couch with her feet tucked under her, she waited for him to bring over the coffee. Her eyebrows rose slightly when she saw the bottle of brandy and two snifters on the tray next to their cups, but she didn't argue when he poured a generous measure for them both. The fiery liquid slid down her throat easily, warming her from within and bolstering her courage to some degree.

She took another, smaller sip before setting the brandy snifter down. "Mikhail . . . I know my turning up like this must seem strange . . . but I really do have a good reason for needing to see you."

Something flashed in his eyes. Concern . . . excitement . . . she wasn't sure which. "I'm sure you do, Erin," he said quietly. "You don't have to convince me of that. Just take your time and tell me what is worrying you."

After the scene in her apartment on New Year's Eve, the last thing she had expected from him was consideration or patience. But he seemed disposed to offer both.

Taking a deep breath, she said slowly, "I found out something today that I'm sure will be a . . . shock to you. . . . It sounds so unbelievable . . . but I'm afraid it's true, and I thought you should know . . . because you're the only one who could—"

His sudden interruption made her break off. "You don't have to say that, Erin. I know I'm the only one."

"Oh . . . well, good . . . I mean it's not as though there aren't other people who will want to help and all that . . . but basically it's going to be up to you to decide what to do."

He frowned slightly. "Up to both of us, don't you mean?" Before she could answer, he went on quickly. "And there really isn't any question of what to do. At least, not as far as I'm concerned. It's my responsibility. After all, I'm the one who was supposed to be making sure that . . ." He stopped, his gaze dark with some emotion that she couldn't fathom. "I'm just very . . . grateful that, after my despicable behavior, you were still willing to come here and tell me."

Puzzled, Erin tried to pin down what it was about his words that confused her. Mikhail seemed already to know what she had come to tell him. Perhaps that meant he had already formulated a plan to defuse the accusations. But what did he mean about it being his responsibility? What had he been supposed to make sure of?

Even as those questions flitted through her mind, they faded before the realization of how he had characterized his actions. Tentatively she murmured, "Does that mean you believe now that there was never anything between Derek and me?"

He nodded gravely. "I think I always knew it, but I was so frightened of my feelings for you that I let my own fears run away with me." Carefully, as though unsure of her response, he reached over and took one of her hands in his. A lean, calloused finger rubbed her palm gently as he said, "Erin, words are inadequate to express how sorry I am for the things I said to you. Believe me, I have berated myself a hundred times since then for being such an insensitive idiot. It isn't possible for you to think worse of me than I do of myself."

"But I don't! That is, I was hurt and angry, of course. But I never stopped . . . I mean . . ." The unmistakable contrition and yearning she saw in his gaze dissolved her last defenses. She could no longer deny her feelings, nor was she willing to try. "I never stopped loving you, Mikhail. I think I've loved you from the moment we met, even though it took me a while to admit it to myself." A soft, wistful smile curved her mouth. "However you feel about me, nothing will ever change that."

"However I . . . ? But I love you. I always have. I took one look at you that afternoon at the airport and thought I had flown straight to heaven." The emotions that she hadn't been able to read in his eyes before were suddenly evident. She saw relief, passion, elation, all intermingling with the glow of deep, abiding love, mirroring her own gaze.

Erin's lips parted on a soundless sigh of pure joy. Hardly daring to believe, she reached out to him shakily. "Mikhail . . . are you sure? That night of the party, I was so worried that you hadn't had a chance to . . . consider alternatives. And then, when I saw you at the gallery with Melinda, I told myself I'd been right . . . that you really did want to go out with other women."

"Foolish angel," he murmured huskily, drawing her into the enchanted circle of his arms. "Melinda is a very kind young lady who took pity on me. She realized immediately that I was in love with someone else and tried her best to convince me that everything would work out. She even helped me find this place. I'm renting it, by the way, with an option to buy. So if you really like it, we can stay here for good." He shook his head ruefully. "I'm afraid I was terrible company for Melinda, especially when I saw you at the art exhibit with that man."

"Sidney? But he's Sheila's husband. They invited

me to go to the gallery with them because I was so down in the dumps about you."

"Ah, that was it. And to think I could cheerfully have strangled him. As it was, I took Melinda home, came back here and did away with the better part of a bottle of vodka." A wry grimace touched his mouth. "I'll never know why that stuff is so popular. It gave me the worst headache I've ever had in my life."

Erin couldn't quite suppress a little chuckle of delight. Happiness beyond anything she had ever imagined glowed within her. "I think we both owe Melinda a vote of thanks. She told me where you were."

"Thank God for that! When I came back here tonight after finding your apartment empty, I didn't know where to look next."

"My apartment? Was that where you were?"

He nodded sheepishly. "You will never know how relieved I was to see you standing outside." His expression grew stern as he added, "But you really should not have waited in the rain. You don't take good enough care of yourself under normal circumstances, but now . . ." A dull flush suffused his cheeks. "Erin, are you very upset about my failure to protect you as well as I thought I was doing?"

Baffled, she shook her head. "Protect? I don't understand. What are you s—?" She broke off suddenly, the meaning of their strangely askewed conversation at last reaching her. *"Oh! You thought . . ."* Swallowing hard, she forced herself to face him. "Mikhail, I didn't come here to tell you I'm pregnant. I'm not . . . at least I don't *think* I am. . . ."

"Then why?" he asked in bewilderment. "What was all that about my being the only one?"

Briefly she explained to him what Derek had told her about the charges being prepared against him. When she was done, Mikhail's eyes were wide with astonishment. He leaned back on the couch, staring at her. "Kent told you this?"

She nodded.

"When?"

"This afternoon, over lunch." Why was he wasting time asking her such questions when he should be concentrating on how best to meet the accusations?

"And that's why you came here?"

"Yes, I just told you. Oh, Mikhail, it's unthinkable that anyone would believe such charges. But I'm afraid that if they're printed there will be some people who'll take them as an excuse to turn against you. Your credibility will be undermined, and you may be subject to all sorts of verbal, even physical, attacks. There has to be something you can do to prevent that."

"Hmmm . . . I see what you mean. Yes, I suppose I really should respond in some way."

"Of course you should!" As he stood up and headed for the phone, she asked anxiously, "What are you going to do?"

"You'll see." He consulted the phone book,

punched out a number and waited a moment before saying, "Ah, good, you're home. It's Demertov. I just called to thank you. . . . Yes, she's here. We've been talking. . . . That's some tale you told her."

He grinned over at Erin, whose eyes were darkening with rapidly growing suspicion. "I owe you quite a favor, but I've no doubt you'll come up with some way to collect. . . . What's that? Melinda? Delightful girl. Listened to me talk about Erin for hours. You know, I couldn't help but notice that the few times I shut up long enough for her to get a word in, you seemed to be on her mind. . . . No, I'm quite sure. . . . That might be a good idea. She'd undoubtedly love to help you celebrate. After all, how often does someone get named editor of the year? Just one thing, though. You should know that she's as intelligent as she is lovely. You won't be able to get away with much."

A low, masculine chuckle reached Erin's burning ears. "Yes, I guess it will make a rather nice change for you. You'll have to bring her to the wedding. Well, I won't keep you. I just wanted you to know how much we both appreciate your . . . creativity."

"That's not what I want to tell him!" Erin began, only to be cut short by Mikhail, who politely made his farewells and hung up. When he turned back to her he was smiling broadly.

"I've completely changed my opinion of Kent. He's not so bad after all."

"He's a con man! He sat there in that restaurant and spun that whole tale of woe about you and that newspaper and . . . ! Oooohhh! How could I have been so stupid? The whole thing was a lie, wasn't it?"

"Not entirely," Mikhail said calmly. "There was an attempt to launch an attack against me using the charges you mention. It happened earlier this week, when I gather you were embroiled with a new assignment and didn't hear about it. The attack fell apart almost before it got started when it was revealed that the so-called witness to my collaboration was an agent of the same regime that was out to discredit me. It was quite an embarrassment for the government of my homeland. My guess is that they will not try anything like it again for fear of drawing even more attention to me and to what I have to say."

"Then . . . you're safe . . . ?"

"Completely. Not that it seemed to matter before you showed up here. Now, however, it means the world." Sitting down beside her, he gently took hold of her clenched hands and drew her close against him. His gaze was infinitely tender as he said, "Erin, I love you with all my heart and soul, and I want you to be my wife."

She swallowed hard, desperate to contain the overpowering surge of joy that spread through every cell of her being. She couldn't let it break free yet, not until she knew. . . . "Even though there may not be any baby?"

Her voice was so low that he had to lean forward to hear her. When he did, he tilted her head back and smiled down at her, his silvery eyes glowing with a fire brighter than any she had ever seen before. "Would you like to have children?"

"Yes . . . your children . . . I love you so. . . ."

"Then you will have to marry me. I am very traditional in that respect. The woman I adore must be my wife before she becomes the mother of our children."

It got very quiet in the room. The only sounds were the splatter of rain against the windows, the crackle of the fire and the soft sighs of lovers.

When Mikhail stood up with her in his arms Erin offered no protest. She snuggled contentedly against his broad chest, listening to the steady beat of his heart as he carried her up the stairs and into his room. A single light burned beside the massive, four-poster bed. By its golden glow they rediscovered each other. The robes fell forgotten to the bed as their hands and lips touched and caressed and savored until the fires of passion raged beyond all control.

Erin cried out softly as he brought them together in unbridled joy. Her body opened to accept his without restraint. They moved as one, climbing higher and higher toward a glimmering peak of pleasure made all the more acute by the knowledge of their mutual love.

When the undulating coils of rapture at last exploded within her, the cry of his name was echoed in her soul. His own being responded an instant later as he joined her in shattering release.

Throughout the long, rain-washed night they came together again and again, setting the seal on a future bright with the promise of abiding love. Not until it was almost morning did they at last drift into a peaceful sleep, nestled in each other's arms, secure in the knowledge that in that embrace they had found the greatest freedom the world could offer.

# 15-Day Free Trial Offer
# 6 Silhouette Romances

**6 Silhouette Romances, free for 15 days!** We'll send you 6 new Silhouette Romances to keep for 15 days, absolutely free! If you decide not to keep them, send them back to us. You pay nothing.

**Free Home Delivery.** But if you enjoy them as much as we think you will, keep them by paying the invoice enclosed with your free trial shipment. We'll pay all shipping and handling charges. You get the convenience of Home Delivery and we pay the postage and handling charge each month.

**Don't miss a copy.** The Silhouette Book Club is the way to make sure you'll be able to receive every new romance we publish before they're sold out. There is no minimum number of books to buy and you can cancel at any time.

This offer expires July 31, 1984

Silhouette Book Club, Dept. SRSE 7L
120 Brighton Road, Clifton, NJ 07012

Please send me 6 Silhouette Romances to keep for 15 days, absolutely free. I understand I am not obligated to join the Silhouette Book Club unless I decide to keep them.

NAME_____

ADDRESS_____

CITY_____ STATE_____ ZIP_____

# MORE ROMANCE FOR
# A SPECIAL WAY TO RELAX
## $1.95 each

| | | | |
|---|---|---|---|
| 2 ☐ Hastings | 23 ☐ Charles | 45 ☐ Charles | 66 ☐ Mikels |
| 3 ☐ Dixon | 24 ☐ Dixon | 46 ☐ Howard | 67 ☐ Shaw |
| 4 ☐ Vitek | 25 ☐ Hardy | 47 ☐ Stephens | 68 ☐ Sinclair |
| 5 ☐ Converse | 26 ☐ Scott | 48 ☐ Ferrell | 69 ☐ Dalton |
| 6 ☐ Douglass | 27 ☐ Wisdom | 49 ☐ Hastings | 70 ☐ Clare |
| 7 ☐ Stanford | 28 ☐ Ripy | 50 ☐ Browning | 71 ☐ Skillern |
| 8 ☐ Halston | 29 ☐ Bergen | 51 ☐ Trent | 72 ☐ Belmont |
| 9 ☐ Baxter | 30 ☐ Stephens | 52 ☐ Sinclair | 73 ☐ Taylor |
| 10 ☐ Thiels | 31 ☐ Baxter | 53 ☐ Thomas | 74 ☐ Wisdom |
| 11 ☐ Thornton | 32 ☐ Douglass | 54 ☐ Hohl | 75 ☐ John |
| 12 ☐ Sinclair | 33 ☐ Palmer | 55 ☐ Stanford | 76 ☐ Ripy |
| 13 ☐ Beckman | 35 ☐ James | 56 ☐ Wallace | 77 ☐ Bergen |
| 14 ☐ Keene | 36 ☐ Dailey | 57 ☐ Thornton | 78 ☐ Gladstone |
| 15 ☐ James | 37 ☐ Stanford | 58 ☐ Douglass | 79 ☐ Hastings |
| 16 ☐ Carr | 38 ☐ John | 59 ☐ Roberts | 80 ☐ Douglass |
| 17 ☐ John | 39 ☐ Milan | 60 ☐ Thorne | 81 ☐ Thornton |
| 18 ☐ Hamilton | 40 ☐ Converse | 61 ☐ Beckman | 82 ☐ McKenna |
| 19 ☐ Shaw | 41 ☐ Halston | 62 ☐ Bright | 83 ☐ Major |
| 20 ☐ Musgrave | 42 ☐ Drummond | 63 ☐ Wallace | 84 ☐ Stephens |
| 21 ☐ Hastings | 43 ☐ Shaw | 64 ☐ Converse | 85 ☐ Beckman |
| 22 ☐ Howard | 44 ☐ Eden | 65 ☐ Cates | 86 ☐ Halston |